GLADFIND AND OTHER MONSTERS

Gladfind and Other Monsters

A Collection of Short Stories

DOUG BROWN

PITTSBURGH:
SERIF PRESS
2026

Cover design by Sophiearts (@SophieAmel35911 on X)

"GladFind" first appeared in *The Pink Hydra*
(https://www.thepinkhydra.com/issues/0101202407/gladfind/)

"Pawns" first appeared in *Half and One*
(https://halfandone.com/pawns/)

"Siobhan's Gathering" first appeared in
Solid Food Press Literary Journal
(https://www.solidfoodpress.com/post/siobhan-s-gathering)

"Spitfire" first appeared in *Half and One*
(https://halfandone.com/spitfire/)

"Strange" first appeared in *Half and One*
(https://halfandonecom/strange/)

In loving memory of Susan, who walked by my side until
I could see the end of two collections.

In thankful memory of Jane, who stood by until I was
ready to take off the training wheels.

Contents

Gladfind

Bartholomew Smoots sat up in his bed, scowling, arms folded across his heaving chest. His bed had been moved several feet closer to the windows. He had liked it where it was. In the far corner of the room stood the closed door to the hallway. A telltale pool of yellow light leaked under the door onto the floor of his room. Occasional interruptions swept from one edge of the door to the other, accompanied by the sounds of his parents going up and down the hall. The yellow light withdrew. His parents had gone to bed. There would be no more changes made tonight. To the right of the hallway door, rounding the corner to the wall opposite his bed, was the closed closet door. Continuing to the right was a bookcase, now in darkness, but Bartholomew knew it was now overstuffed with his toys and books. To his left, on his nightstand sat the teddy-bear lamp with glowing balloon night-light. There were now matching sippy cups for water on either side of the lamp. And on the far side of the nightstand stood the new bed that had appeared out of nowhere and a second bookcase which was not new but now empty except for a diaper-changing tray, a new star-covered soccer ball, and three books that supposedly Bartholomew would have no more use for: *Hop on Pop*, *Goodnight Moon*, and *The Very Hungry Caterpillar*. I don't know why anyone would think I wouldn't have use for those books anymore, thought Bartholomew. Those are perfectly good books. I can still get joy out of them. Lots of joy. Oodle-buckets of joy. I really would have *loved* to read those books *today*. But *someone* moved them. Maybe tomorrow I'll move them back to the other bookcase—yes. Bartholomew looked back at the other bed, glaring. He slid down under his covers and turned to face the window.

With one ear buried in the pillow, he could still hear some sounds of the house and his parents settling in for the night—sounds becoming more distant and less definite. Slowly, he became more conscious of the sounds of the room. And gradually, he began to focus on background sounds of the house itself—the graceless flatulence of the heating vents, the unsettled gurgling of the water heater somewhere in the house's bowels, the creak and groan of old timbers and weary joints. And then, the muffled sounds began to reach his other ear, transmitted through the bed frame, the mattress, and his pillow—sounds both indistinct and yet distinctly different from those of the house. Tapping. And scraping. Like a mouse. Or some other uninvited nocturnal visitor. Or perhaps an unauthorized resident.

That sound was *definitely* back—the sound that he thought he had heard so often, indistinctly. But now there was no doubt. It was coming from under his bed—a sound like maybe plastic scraping on wood, tooth on metal, claw on tile.

Bartholomew grabbed his flashlight from under his pillow and slowly leaned his head over the side of his bed, trying not to make a sound. Then he clicked on his light. In a flash, he saw something smaller than a squirrel, larger than a chipmunk, dash along the wall at the head of his bed and cower by the far side, its head bobbing like a prize fighter or a bobble-head baseball player.

Almost as soon as his light had flashed on, his weight cascaded over the edge of the bed and he ended up lying on his side on the floor, in a pool of silvery evening light from the window. Sprawled on the floor, he instinctively trained the flashlight once again on the monster under the bed. It had a fuzzy reindeer-snowflake sock for a body with a black elastic hair ribbon as a belt and a used vanilla pudding cup to cover its head. It brandished a JoJo's FroYo spork and presented a cozy war-like visage. It turned away, as if collecting itself, and then turned back suddenly for effect, shouting, "Habubabub-abah!" He made a show of shaking his spork in Bartholomew's direction. "Hubah!" he continued, "Hubaah!" It then seemed to sag and stood spent under its pudding cup. His head began bobbling noticeably and finally stopped. After an awkward moment, he spoke in a tone both diminutive and brash, saying, "You wouldn't have come across my shield in the last few days, would you? It says, 'Braunschwieger Delicatessen' on it." After another pause, he continued testily, "You *can* read, can't you?"

Bartholomew propped his head up on his elbow and answered flatly, choosing not to take offense at the small monster's tone. "I can read, but I can't read what you said."

"Understandable. My shield is not a toy. Not a child's plaything. It's a piece of military armament. I wouldn't expect you to know about such things." The little figure looked around the under-bed realm. "It's white with a picture of a cow's head on it. Says, 'lite sour cream.' "

Bartholomew addressed the monster brusquely and directly. "Are you the monster that lives under my bed?" He accosted the small figure as if offended by his presence. "The one who makes such an awful racket when I'm trying to sleep? Who waits until the house is quiet and then starts scraping and tapping on the floor and the wall like you're trying to find a secret trap door?"

"I guess so. I'm the only one under this bed, you know." He moved slightly as if shifting his weight from one foot to another. "You've never really looked, have you?"

"To be honest, you sounded so scary. I was kinda scared to look."

"And what? I don't look as scary as I sounded?"

"Well, yuh, and when I shine my light on you, you look even less scary."

"That is a challenge to monster-kind. Taking a good, hard look often diminishes the scare factor. And often the more light, the smaller we look. Don't even get me started on the effects of daylight."

"You're really not so big, you know. You're not so scary."

He instantly stiffened, standing erect. "I'll have you know, I am tremendously fiercesome and fiercesomely tremendous."

"There's no such thing as 'fiercesomely tremendous,'" Bartholomew challenged.

"Sure, there is." He took a small step forward, waving his spork, as if offering himself for examination. "Just look at me. First, I'm tremendous, no doubt. A tremendous monster, am I. That's undeniable. For one. And second, I'm fiercely so. You've never met a fiercer monster than me, I'll bet you any amount. Certainly, you haven't met any under *this* bed. You haven't, have you? Come now. Admit it."

"Well, . . . I used to be afraid of you, I'll admit. What with your scratching and scraping and gnawing and gnashing."

"That would be me sharpening my terrible, swift spork and polishing my great and sturdy shield. . . which I would show you if I could find it." He twisted from side to side.

Bartholomew looked at him with puzzlement and the weariness of unwelcome age. "I admit, I used to be afraid of your noises, your dashing and scurrying about under the bed. I don't have that luxury anymore. I'm now a big brother. *I'm* Bartholomew Smoots. And my little brother, Maximillian Smoots, will be moving out of the nursery and into this room and a big-boy bed any day now." Saying that outloud seemed to change his demeanor. "That bed over there," and he gestured wearily with his chin toward the bed on the other side of the room.

The sock monster looked across to the other bed and said, "Oh, very nice indeed, indeed." Momentarily, he seemed to turn his pudding cup to compare the under-realms of the two beds. Then turning his focus back to Bartholomew, he continued, "I suppose you'll be on to big-brother games and adventures." His stature seemed to sag. "I can't scare you with battle cries and war dances, I suppose. Hmm."

They shared a thought-heavy silence. And then Bartholomew took the initiative, stepping into his new role. "I will have to be the brave one. I have to *be* that. I have to spot danger and steer Max away from it." His voice trailed off thoughtfully. And then Bartholomew gathered himself, as if resigned to the need to be brave, and said in a bold but shaky voice, "What is your name, monster?"

The sock monster bristled and looked directly at him, but he remained defiantly silent.

"As lord of this domain, I command you to tell me your name!" A palpable silence filled the room. "In the name of the House of Smoots, I command thee!"

The underling sidled back and forth in resignation and then said, "Sire, I am Gladfind, a sock gnome of the dryer tribe. Ever since escaping from the dryer, I have freely roamed and ransacked this household only to become trapped by a series of cunning enchantments that have imprisoned me under this very big-boy bed."

"What if I just grab you and put you back in the laundry?" Bartholomew asked, glibly, full of false bluster.

He bowed his head and answered in a subdued tone, "I would cease to exist." Silence hung in the air.

"That hardly seems like a desirable or gentlemanly step to take, then." Bartholomew paused, thinking, he doesn't seem like a very scary monster at all. "But I do have to make sure this room is safe for my baby brother before he moves in. I can't have him jumping into my bed to escape some minor gremlin or hobgoblin. He has his own bed. Let him stay in it."

"Well, sire, you should probably deal with the monster in the closet, then. He's the real threat to you and your little brother. And he's been growing in recent weeks. At an alarming rate."

He looked out beyond the foot of his bed to where he could see that the closet door was ajar. He was sure it had been closed when he climbed into bed. Shining his flashlight on it, he could see a deep darkness between the door jamb and the edge of the door. "Gladfind," he asked, "you seem to be familiar with the monster in the closet. Do you know what kind of monster he might be? Do you know who that monster is?"

"Sire," he began, "I'm afraid I know a lot about that monster that lurks in your closet, and I'm afraid that none of it is good." After he spoke, Gladfind began to bobble back and forth. "And he has many names. He can take many forms, because he has many ways of attacking the Truth and those who belong to the Truth."

"Gladfind, why are you bobbling like that?'

"Sorry, sire, but I felt a chill. And I have no spine."

"You're scared?"

"No, sire, never. Except, sometimes. And in this case, yes."

"You're scared to talk about the closet monster?"

"Scared that he might hear me talking about him. He doesn't take kindly to it. He's full-on agitated by hearing the truth. It's the one thing he can't stand."

"You're scared by what you know about the closet monster?"

"I'm scared about what he does to misplaced toys and stray playing cards and . . . and, yes, what he does to sock gnomes."

"But you said you were tremendously fierce?"

"Well, yes. I wield a mighty blade called SpiritSong that was forged generations ago in the very bowels of this house."

"Sock gnome generations?"

"Uh, yes."

"What's the lifespan of a sock gnome?"

"Sometimes a week, sometimes as long as ten months?"

"And you say your spork was forged in this house?"

"Well, I picked it out of the garbage, so —." He began to bobble once again, and then straightened up. "But as I was saying, I carry the shield Fidelis that has guarded the hearts and heads of many of the gnomes of my line."

"OK."

"And my loins are girded with the belt of Truth and Verity."

"You have loins?" Then redirecting his flashlight, "It looks like a scrunchy with sparkles."

Gladfind took a sudden step forward as if for emphasis. "And this," he said tapping his pudding cup with his spork, "is the helmet of Safery."

"Safery?"

"Many of the good names were taken, sire."

"That's all very well and good," Bartholomew said, "but you know the sound of you is really much scarier than the sight of you."

"Truth, my liege. That Dragon's Breath that you carry," and he gestured toward my flashlight, "is really much mightier than my trusty SpiritSong, though she has certainly gotten me out a many a scrape in the gnome-scape of Smoots."

"Fine. So, you point to the monster in the closet. Why is he so scary? You *are* a real monster, aren't you?"

"Ye-es." And he seemed to swallow, as much as a sock gnome is able to swallow. And then he began to recite, slowly, "The monster in your closet is the fiercest variety of monster. He's a *phantasm*. He's not visible if you look directly at him. He'll approach you when you're not looking. He'll attack you from the side, the back. He will sneak up beside you and whisper in your ear. He wants to *destroy* you and your dominion. He wants to bring down the mighty House of Smoots. Sock gnomes like me are fierce, yes, oh, so fierce, but oh, so noble, and worthy of glory, though a little envious . . . and occasionally jealous . . . and at our worst covetous—only at our worst are we covetous, and very petty. We just want what you have. And we think we deserve it.

Yes, we deserve it. We're fascinated by the things that humans have and make and create. And we can't create like that, what with socks having no thumbs, so we are left to inhabit your possessions and the work of your hands. Our greatest joy is to grab something that you have poured yourself into and inhabit that something. But a phantasm wants to destroy you and take over your rightful place in Eternity. He'll try to deceive you. He's a liar and a cheat. A fraudster. He'll tell you the smallest half-truths and the littlest whitest lies, and if you fall for his fiblings, you will be trapped, ensnared, enslaved. The ultimate lie is that you will be free if you'll do just one thing he asks." He breathed in and continued, "If you hear him whispering in your ear, and you try to look at him, he'll phantasm. You can't see him. But if you practice looking along the edges, you'll be able to see him crouching, wringing his hands, always straightening out his old suit with the shiny elbows and knees and always trying to look over your shoulder, trying to see what you're reading, what you're playing with, trying to figure out what's most important to you."

Gladfind fell silent and began to bobble and bobbled faster and faster, staring at a point just to Bartholomew's right.

What Bartholomew heard next was a whisper that began like a rake collecting dry leaves and ended like an icy wind. It said, "If you hear him whispering in your ear, and you try to look at him, he'll phantasm. You can't see him. But he'll breathe in your so-o-o-o-o-ul." Bartholomew sensed something directly behind him as he lay on the floor. He tried to turn his head quickly to catch a glimpse of whatever it was, but instead he flopped over onto his back, looking up at the ceiling. In the moonlight that came in the window, he glimpsed a wispy vapor rising toward the ceiling and then turning out of sight. Immediately, Bartholomew scrambled up into bed and the safety of his covers.

The door to the hallway opened, driving a slim spike of yellow light into the room pointing to the empty bed. "Bart?" came a whisper. Mother's face pushed into the room. "Bart, honey, stay in bed. You hear? You'll wake up Max."

"Yes, Mum." Bartholomew nodded in the dim light. The door closed. The pool of light on the floor and the other bed withdrew beneath the door.

Clutching his covers securely around his neck, Bartholomew turned onto his stomach and called over the side of the bed in a half-whisper, "Gladfind. Gladfind, can you hear me?"

"Yes, sire," came a fuzzy, blustery voice from underneath the bed.

"What else do you know about this phantasm thing?"

"He's a usurper, Sire."

"What's a *usurper*."

"Sire, he's like a snake. And he wants to take your place. He loves the things you don't use every day, the things you stop paying attention to. He'll settle into your wellies or your galoshes and hide behind your umbrella. He'll nestle into your winter coats in the summer and your rain slicker in the winter. He'll try to act like they belong to him and trick you into thinking that they're rightfully his. He'll try to convince you to leave or get you kicked out if he can."

As Bartholomew peered down over the side of the bed, a voice of despair came from behind his head, saying, "Pay no mind to Gladfind. He's just an empty *sock*." Bartholomew looked quickly to his left and saw only emptiness. The voice now came from behind him. "An empty sock." Jerking his neck back to the right, he again heard from behind his head, "Empty sock." Bartholomew pulled his head back under his covers completely. He counted to ten and peeked out.

Again, armed with his flashlight, Bartholomew moved under the covers to the other side of his own bed, now facing the other bed. He pointed the light at the closet door, which now stood open almost halfway. As he moved the flashlight's beam around the interior of the closet, his boots and coats made shadows that seemed to retreat from him, each pinned up against the back of the closet, trying to hide behind a boot or coat. As he moved the beam away from the closet, Bartholomew thought he heard someone exhale. Flashing back to the closet, he saw nothing but some clothes swinging.

Bartholomew looked back down over the edge of the bed and called in a hoarse whisper, "Gladfind! Gladfind!"

The dry voice returned behind his ear. "Mother loves Maximillian *very* much. Maybe she won't have any love left for *you*."

Bartholomew looked around the room as he called under the bed. "Gladfind! Can you hear me?"

"Yes, sire!" came the small fuzzy voice from under the bed, accompanied by scraping sounds, and then sounds of plastic tapping on plastic. "*There's* my mighty Veritas!" And again, he made a tapping sound, like plastic tapping on plastic.

"Gladfind, what should I do? Can I chase him out? How do you defeat a phantasm?"

"You can't defeat him by fighting him. He's too crafty. Too cunning. He's a master of the use of half-truths. He'll lead you astray and then you'll be lost."

"Yes, but I'm the big brother. I need to make this room safe for Maximillian."

"You drive him back with truth and light. Lead with your mighty Dragon's Breath, and then follow with what you know to be true. Absolute truth. With confidence. Be bold and courageous, and he will flee. You defeat him by making his half-truths irrelevant."

Shining his flashlight around the room, he now saw the closet door standing three-quarters of the way open. Shining his light into the closet, he again saw nothing but swaying clothes. Shining his light off the mirror on the back of the hallway door, the light beam reflected off the mirror and struck the open closet door, revealing a shadow that took the shape of a large rodent, much like an opossum, but wearing a suit of clothes, crouching on his hind legs, and wringing his hands, his front paws.

"Gladfind, I'm scared."

"You're wise to be scared. But being courageous is not about *not* being scared. You just have to be confident that you're doing the *right* thing, *even though* it's scary."

A yellow light appeared under the hallway door. Footsteps flip-flopped down the hall. The door opened and Bartholomew's mother entered the room. Taking several steps in, she reached the closet door and firmly closed it. She took several steps toward Bart's bed and leaned down to kiss him good night. "Now go to sleep, little man," she said insistently. And she retreated from the room, closing the door behind her. The yellow light under the door withdrew as the sound of her slippers receded.

Bartholomew slowly slid out of his bed and stood looking directly at the closed closet door. The door slowly opened.

He heard a rustling like a November breeze moving dry leaves.

Bartholomew gathered himself and spoke into the darkness, "That's not your closet. This isn't your room. I want you out of here, in the name of the House of Smoots! You will not touch me! You are a liar. A usurper." Bartholomew paused and thought he heard a faint laugh. He continued with a new sense of purpose. "You will not touch Maximillian! My mother loves him! My mother loves me! My father loves both of us! And I command you to leave! Now!" Bartholomew's body quivered as his voice rose. A sound arose from the closet like shoes and books being knocked about. Hangers could be heard banging against each other. A shoebox fell from the top shelf. A voice gave an audible, "Hmmph!"

Bartholomew, with trusty Dragon's Breath in hand, stood alone in the center of the room and moved slowly forward. He reached out to the knob of the closet door. He could hear sounds of angry scuffling from inside the closet. Turning the knob and throwing the door open, he shined his light into the bottom of the closet. The light bounced off boots and boxes. He focused his eyes on the threshold and he could make out in the center of the commotion one small rodent-faced creature dressed in a shabby black suit worn smooth on the knees and elbows, fuming and fussing, shriveling and shrinking, staring up at Bartholomew and stamping his feet. And then turning and staring, he pointed one rat-like finger and shrieked, "You not perfect. And you *don't* deserve to be loved. And you *aren't* loved." His accusations fell flat, and then he was gone.

A small fuzzy voice came from beneath the bed. "Sire. Remember. He's not gone just because you can't see him.

He's always looking for new lies and half-truths to use to bring you down. He's never gone. He's just waiting for a time when you don't expect him."

And then all was quiet.

A yellow light appeared under the hallway door. The doorknob turned and Bartholemew's mother entered the room once again. "Bart. Into bed, you silly!" She yawned. "Whatever are you doing?" She closed the closet door and then steered him by the shoulders toward the bed. He scrambled under the covers and she leaned over to kiss him good night. "Love you. Now good night." She went back out the door, pulling it closed behind her. The yellow light withdrew leaving silence. And soon a faint scraping noise of plastic on plastic could be heard under the bed.

The Ghost Of Granma Herbert

John-John's window faces east, and he's usually up with the sun. He's generally the first one awake in the Haggertys' third-floor apartment, and out of his fine human instinct for self-preservation, he's grown into the habit of playing quietly in his room until the rest of the family is up and about. This morning he's working his newest trick—opening the window screen. He still can't get the one on the right window; it's too hard for his not-quite-five-year-old hands to work the latch springs. But the other one's not as stiff, and he goes at it whenever Mother isn't looking of listening. It's a feat of strength for him, like opening the car door.

He drags over the kiddy-chair that goes wit his kiddy-desk. Standing on the chair he's at the right level to put all his weight into the effort. The screen is up in two seconds. Leaning out the window, his tummy on the windowsill, he scouts the half-lit landscape—the house next door, the driveway that runs between houses, the long sloping half-wooded backyard to his right, and to his left the road that cuts to within twenty feet of the building's foundation.

John-John slides off the chair and scrambles back to the bed. He orders a bomber strike. He taxis his bomber fleet along the bedspread. Working as his own ground crew, he jumps down and pulls out a handful of great, big bombs from his secret armory beneath the bureau. He loads the bomb bay and takes off on a dawn bombing raid. The enemy is sighted, not directly below. The first wave tosses its deadly cargo of road gravel and garden stones. The strike misses—too far out. The enemy cat freezes in fear.

But now that his microphone hand is free again, radio contact is reestablished. The bombardiers adjust their sightings. This time the strike is a success. The cat burns and smokes as it darts away to its home across the driveway. Mission Accomplished. The victorious bomber flight returns to base, crash-landing on the bed.

The door opens and Mother's early-morning crab-face destroys his world of make-believe. The battlefield is gone. There is only John-John on his bed, a kiddy-chair by an open window, and Mother's sqinty-eyed pruneface in the door.

At first the wrinkles go the right way. "Breakfast, Tiger," she says.

But a guilty look gives him away, and a quick glance around the room turns the wrinkles all the wrong way. The voice gets gruff and loud, and John-John wishes he weren't even there. "Have you been at that window again?!" it rumbles. John-John doesn't like it when the voice gets loud and gruff. "How many times have I told you?! Do you know you could get hurt?! Fall out and smash your head on the sidewalk?!"

Mother marches him into the kitchen for breakfast, using her Hard Hand, the one that always follows the Mad Voice.

Though Mother scares him at times, she still seems to be the source of everything—all strength and power and any warmth and affection. John-John thinks of her as super. John-John's older brother, Ray, Jr., calls her domineering and over-bearing. But those words don't mean much to John-John. He settles for super.

His oatmeal arrives in front of him, and the Mad Voice goes off to call Daddy, Ray, Jr., and Pheobe, who each arrive in turn, each more or less prune-faced, each more of less squinty-eyed. None of them like to play in the morning.

But Daddy doesn't stay long, and he doesn't say much to Mother. Mother and Daddy fought last night about a trash-can lid. So, Daddy eats toast and drinks coffee, and rushes off to build more airplanes. He's an engineer, though he doesn't drive a train. And he works for BOAC, which isn't a word, even though it's made up of letters. John-John thinks Daddy is super.

Mother keeps filling and refilling John-John's cereal bowl and milk glass, as well as Pheobe's. Ray, Jr., serves himself. Little Ray has on his new work boots and work pants he bought just for his summer job. He sweeps the Stern's stock room at the Paramus Mall, which isn't a bad job for a kid fresh out of junior high. Of course, Mother says that the job hardly requires uniform pants and work boots—"Jeans and sneakers would be just fine," she keeps saying—but Ray really wants to look his best—"You want me to grow up to be a slob?!" he keeps responding. Ray seems to worry a lot about what other people think of him.

John-John really works at getting as much cereal as possible onto his spoon, into his mouth, and down into his stomach. He derives a great sense of pride from mastering each new skill, and he also wants very much to grow as big and strong as Daddy so he can cross the street by himself and go into the bank and get money.

Pheobe, however, seems to enjoy annoying people. She is a near-perfect brat. She's just now learning to make popping noises when she chews her gum, and she practices the trick for all to hear and see. She sits at the table, just to the right of Mother, directly across from John-John. She swings her legs and chews her oatmeal with her mouth open, making a squishy "Phloosh" sound as she bobs up and down, John-John is occasionally bothered by the shin-crack of a stray foot, which causes him to shout involuntarily. Ray, Jr., seems occasionally bothered by the sight of her half-chewed food, which causes him to whine. Pheobe boasts about the power she wields over "two mere men."

"Ray, honey," Mother tries to coo in her early-morning gravel-voice, "can't you stop worrying about your sister's manners? She's well on her way to becoming a perfect lady."

The show of the near-perfect lady-brat again cracks into the tender shin of the youngest, who gives another involuntary "Ooch!" even though he tries his best to keep it in. He knows men don't cry—or go "Ooch!"

"John-John," Mother gravel-coos, "what's wrong? Hiccup?"

"N-Ooch." He glares across the table. "Pee-pee's kicking me!" he blurts out in a moment of weakness. And Mother gets mad.

"How many times must I tell you?! Pronounce it right or don't say it at all, OK?!" It has been cute the first time he's said it, but cute wears off fast, John-John has learned. But it still makes Phoebe mad. "Apologize," Mother says.

John-John glares across the table. "Sorry I called you Peepee." But this only brings back the Hard Hand, across his face this time.

"Say it right." The Hard Hand is ready.

"Phoe-pee!" The Hard Hand, followed by kiddy-screaming.

"Say it right!"

"Phoeeeeee-beeeeeee-yahhhhhh-ahahhhhhhhh."

Ray, Jr., excuses himself and hurries off to catch the bus for work—a half-hour early.

Vindicated, Phoebe goes into the living room to lie down in front of the TV. She's asleep again in twenty minutes—she only gets up at 6:30 because sleeping late means going all morning without breakfast. "If you give one of the 'em special treatment, they'll all want special treatment," Mother says. Mother says a lot of things like that. She's smart.

By and by, John-John stops crying. He's down the stairs and outside as soon as Mother pulls a sweatshirt over him and lets him out the door. But he has to stay in the backyard where Mother can see him from the kitchen window.

The backyard is dewy-damp and cold in its dawn shadows. Beads of water sparkle on a few blades of grass, a few leaves of trees, the neighbor's chain-link fence. Every bit of the yard is ever-new to John-John, though Mother sees many causes for worry. Mother tells him, for instance, that trees in the back yard get hungry when it gets dark. He's never seen the trees eat anyone or anything. But Mother says so.

Another thing John-John knows is that cats are bad. Mother gets sick from them, scratching and sneezing. "They are very bad," Mother said once and repeats every so often. "They can kill you just like they killed Granma Herbert."

Once, Ray, Jr., told him that Granma Herbert was still alive. He said she went to see the Nile—or something. She sits, seeing what's not there, talking to listeners who aren't there, thinking thoughts that she thought long ago. She's cared for, Ray, Jr., says. John-John believes Ray, Jr., but believes Mother more. Mother says Granma Herbert has gone "over there," because of the "cat-marks," the awful hives she's had when he's last seen her. She's scratched them till they bled, without noticing the blood on her hands. And it was all because of the cats.

The other neighbors, the ones without the fence and the terrier, have cats. The two families that live below the Haggertys have no cats, no terriers. The second-floor people have a girl—an old one with tits. Ray, Jr., has told him about tits. The first-floor people have no girl. But they own the building, and they're real old. John-John doesn't worry about any of these things. He doesn't worry about anything. Unless Mother says to.

John-John rides his Big-Wheel in and out of the garage, around the driveway, pretending he's Daddy. The girl with the tits walks out to the garage. She's on her way to work.

"Hi, John-John," she says. John-John thinks she's pretty. He used to think she was a nice lady, but he heard Mother talking about her once. "That girl's a painted lady," she'd say, "and mark my word, she'll end up a scarlet woman," whatever that meant. The girl gives people manicures at the Cosmetic Connection out at the Mall. She offered to drive Ray, Jr., to work this summer, but Mother made him refuse, because she worries about him associating with the wrong crowd.

The girl backs her red Mustang our of the garage, and she waves to John-John as she pulls away. John-John pedals around the driveway a while because the dark garage is shadow-cold. But the driveway gets hot, driving him back into the cool garage.

He's still the only kid playing outside. Soon other kids will come out, maybe coming over to play with him, maybe calling John-John over to play with them. But he doesn't mind being alone in the early morning, because he's a morning person, and this is a beautiful morning. The sun is almost everywhere.

Now that the red car is gone from the garage, John-John can see the trash cans and the lid that Mother and Daddy fought over. The lid lies next to the cans, because it's now too bent to fit them. Mother bent it up last night. She'd taken out some trash and found a cat upsetting one of the cans. She had tried, several times, to hit it with the lid, but mostly she just bent the lid up to the cement floor. John-John had been helping her take the trash out, and all the noise had frightened him. But Mother told him it was a good thing to do. All sweaty from the effort, she'd looked down at him and said with a smile, "It's a lousy job, but someone's gotta do it." And later Daddy yeller at her and she'd yelled back. John-John knew that Daddy was always right, but Mother was always more right.

John-John stops his Big-Wheel to look at the lid. He gathers up his courage to pick it up and look under it. He just touches it the first time and jumps away. The second time he lifts it up partway but drops it as he bends over to look under it. The third time he does it, he looks. There's nothing there, nothing to be afraid of, though he knows there very well could have been.

Losing interest, he drops the lid and looks around the dusty garage. A piece of brick catches his eye. It's about three quarters of a five-pound red brick. It looks new, with sharp corners and smooth sides. There's even a sort of shine to its surface—except on the cut side. It's a beautiful brick. John-John can think of a zillion great things to do with such a nice brick. But he decides first of all to smuggle it into the house; he might want to use it with his building set or something. Anyway, his mission is to get the precious red gold into the royal treasure vault that holds his shoes and shirts and pants and things. The Empire will go broke without the precious gold.

First, John-John sets out on foot to scout the whereabouts of the marauding renegade Mother, who would kill to get her hands on the precious red gold and keep it from saving the Empire. He finds her, conveniently enough, in the laundry room in the basement. His mission will be relatively easy, but there isn't a moment to lose. In true super-spy fashion, John-John lugs his prize brick unseen into the building and up the countless steps, one by one. He doesn't know how many there are. He's counted as many as fifteen, but he knows there are more like fifty or a hundred. Only the dreaded Phoebe remains to be dealt with now. But he catches it asleep, and he slips into his room. The Empire has been saved and John-John can breathe easier.

John-John goes back outside, and the rest of the morning drifts by in similar amusements. John-John is surprised to hear Mother hollering him in for lunch already. Lunch is a food, a time of day, and a seating arrangement. John-John thinks word games are great.

After lunch comes nap time. Mother tucks John-John in and tells him to "nap nice and let Mommy rest some." But he doesn't feel like napping, and as he lies there staring toward the window, he feels the urge to work the window screen. He decides that letting Mother rest is what's important, so as long as he's quiet, he reasons, he'll still be good. Ever so quietly he drags over the kiddy-chair that goes with his kiddy-desk. Ever so quietly and ever so slowly he pulls the window latches on either side of the screen and lifts the screen. Leaning out the window, his tummy on the windowsill, he scans the sun-lit view. The world is really pretty now, and the warm air carries the thick scents of the beautiful weeds and flowers that grow in the garden along the side of the house and around the back door. There's movement almost everywhere now—cars, planes, birds, and cats. There's one right down there by the peonies. And it's lazily strolling this way.

Instantly, military intelligence calls battle-stations. The bomber fleet is aloft at a moment's notice. But this time there is only one bomber. And it carries the Fat Bomb—he'd seen a picture of it in one of Ray's big schoolbooks.

The bombardier sights over the windowsill. The enemy is almost directly below him now. "Bombs away!" and the bomb load is sent hurtling, spinning, twirling just like a real bomb in a real war movie. A second later, the brick lands as if it had eyes. The cat that had been strolling so lazily just a second earlier has stopped strolling. Is has almost stopped doing anything. The most devastating bombing run in recorded history.

But he hears Mother moving about again, so he goes out into the hall, acting like he's just woken up, and he asks her to let him go outside again. He doesn't tell Mother, but there's something really neat he wants to go see. He's down the stairs in record time.

He knows Mother wants him to stay in the back. But he has to get around to the side of the house. And Mother sees him from the kitchen window and sets out down the stairs with the intention of teaching him a lesson.

When John-John gets to the scene of the destruction, he sees that the enemy is still breathing. It breathes slowly, struggling to force air in and out of its crushed ribcage. One paw waves feebly, as it the cat can crawl out from under the brick. It looks sad. It doesn't seem to blame John-John. And it doesn't seem bad at all. In fact, it's soft. And it makes nice noises when he touches it. But the noises get quieter. And then they stop.

John-John kneels by the body, and though the midday noises continue around him, he senses a strange still and a disturbing quiet. He fails to notice Mother as she storms around the corner of the house and heads intently toward the stooping boy. But her tense, red-mad face softens and lightens when she makes out the object of his interest. Mother seems nothing short of proud of John-John's work. She excuses him for it most big-heartedly. She glows with the thought that her tireless efforts to raise her boy right have paid off.

She kneels down taking John-John in her arms and cuddling him, pressing his little torso to her breast and his little head to her collarbone, rocking him slowly from side to side, murmuring more to herself than to him, pressing, rocking, murmuring.

John-John does nothing. He wants to cry for some reason, but he can't. It's not a time for tears. It's a time for seeing things as they are. All John-John can see are patches of cat and bloody grass and a dizzy, rocking sky. All he can feel is the smothering pressure of Mother's body pinning his arms to his sides and burying his mouth and nose in her shoulder. And all he can hear is the low drone of Mother's voice, drowning out all other sound.

On Toppa the Heap

Ginny put down her fork, picked up her plate and sighed, "Rondo, bedtime." Rondo recognized it as a necessary kindness, not a punishment. It was early—still plenty of daylight—but his father, Brian, wasn't home yet. When Brian got home after seven, he was usually loud and wobbly and bleary-eyed. He could be a little angry or a little emotional—for no apparent reason. He'd say things or break things and then blame it on other people. "Look what you made me do!" Rondo had some sketchy memories that would come back to him in dreams—someone locked behind the bathroom door, someone pulling on the doorknob, someone punching a wall. He had clearer memories of Brian on his knees crying like a baby, "Never again, I swear, never again." Rondo hated this lack of control—this weakness. He vowed to never be the weak one. He would be the strong one, the one who called the shots.

On this particular night, Ginny cleared the table including the butter dish and the salt and pepper shakers, even the napkin tray—less to throw. She ushered Rondo off to his room. She tucked him in and kissed him good night while listening nervously for the sound of the front door. The fragrances of basil and mint and Cashmere Bouquet embraced Rondo and then receded as Ginny pulled the door shut behind her.

Rondo listened momentarily to the sounds of the house. Their apartment was the second floor of a triple-decker. No sound came from the upstairs apartment—no one home. The woman downstairs, the widowed landlady, clinked dishes and clashed silverware and by the sound of it she was heading to the kitchen. Rondo could make out faint sounds of dishes being washed in the wide porcelain sink.

Rondo's room was at the front of the house—a converted sleeping porch that had been closed in a generation or two earlier. The outside wall had once been all screens allowing the cool night air to create a bearable place to sleep during the hot summer nights. Now it was a wall of aluminum-framed double-hung windows. His bed was pushed up against the front windows that ran the full width of the wide but shallow room. The head of his bed had pillows stacked up in one corner. On hot summer nights, Ginnie would raise the bottom sashes as far as they would go, letting in as much night air as possible to cool off the room.

On this March night, the panes were cold to the touch. Rondo rolled over toward the wall of windows and bunched his pillows up so his chin could clear the windowsill. He pushed the metal window frame up until there was enough space to lean his cheek against the cold metal screen. He could hear the sounds of the street and look beyond the foot of his bed down the block as far as the Stallion Bar 'N' Grill at the corner. People called it the Black Stallion because of its black faux marble siding. The traffic light flashed from yellow to red, and Rondo could make out the shapes of neon beer signs in the small windows of the bar—the "Carling Black Label" maple leaf, "Narragansett" with the oldie-style sailing ship, and "Ballantine Beer" with the three rings. It was still too early for the neon lights to command the indifferent twilight. Holding his finger up to the mesh screen, Rondo traced the shape of the Ballantine sign—a golden neon pretzel. He could make out familiar music which grew louder whenever someone went in or out of the bar. A shadow stood at the corner of the building—one of Giacco's men—his driver. The music crescendoed as patrons entered or exited: "I wanna be a part of," and then moments later, "On toppa the heap!" An arm emerged from inside the bar and held open the door: "If. I. Can." Someone emerged silver-haired in a fur-trimmed camel coat—Giacco himself. Two more men, stocky and dour, one dark-haired, one balding, followed him and then flanked him as he moved toward the street. Giacco nodded to the shadow at the corner of the building. The shadow peeled off the building and strode gingerly toward the black Cadillac Fleetwood parked at the opposite curb. The shadow circled around to the far curbside and opened the rear door for Giacco. The other two diverged. Dark hair slid into the street-side rear door. Balding followed Giacco and took shotgun. That's what they called the front passenger seat, because on westerns like *The Way the West Was Won* or *Maverick* a man would sit alongside the driver of a stagecoach or wagon with a shotgun to fend off marauders. Doors slammed and the car pulled out from the curb and eased down the street. It floated by Rondo's window, and Rondo momentarily locked eyes with Shotgun who pointed the sign of a finger pistol up at Rondo followed by an imperceptible nod. As the car passed, Rondo craned his neck to follow it. He finally had to raise up on his arm to turn his head. He pressed his other cheek against the screen. A half block further, the car pulled abreast of an indistinct figure and stopped. The rear window came down. Something was said, some deep rumbling. Then everything seemed to stop. Rondo held his breath to listen. The figure on the sidewalk turned his head, looked skyward, perhaps looking for a savior, more likely searching for one more excuse, hoping to delay the inevitable. His voice sounded like a mouse. Shotgun emerged from the car, put an arm around the shrinking figure and steered him silently around the back of the car and into the driver's side rear door. Now Rondo, still holding his breath, could hear Shotgun's footsteps distinctly crunching on the pavement as he made his way back around the car and pulled his door shut behind him. The car sped off down the street.

Suddenly Rondo heard the sound of a key in the lock of the front door downstairs; the rattle and squeak of the mailbox; the familiar rising timbre of his father's footsteps on the front stairs approaching their apartment. Rondo could hear Ginny moving to greet him—moving halfway to the door. "Brian?" The thin voice rose.

Brian's voice sounded clear and upbeat, though muffled.

Ginny's voice responded lower, fuller, relieved.

Rondo kicked out of his covers and slid out of bed. He padded over to his door and listened at the keyhole. The voices came through as if at the far end of a tunnel.

"I got the job." Brian's voice was hushed but excited.

"You got it?!"

"I got it!!" The voice was raised but in a good way.

Rondo heard sounds of some kind of movement.

"I'll tell Rondo in the morning at breakfast."

"Brian, we're getting out of this crumby place!" The voices continued, talking fast and low, growing indistinct as they moved through the apartment.

The next morning, Brian shared with Rondo that Brian had been offered a new job and he'd be leaving his old job. Brian was going from doing a job Rondo had never seen in a place Rondo had never been to doing a new job in another place that Rondo had never been. Whatever.

Some days later, a truck pulled up in front of the house. Four men in grey overalls climbed out, mechanically loaded every single thing in the apartment into cardboard boxes of every conceivable size and shape, carried the boxes one at a time, two at a time, three at a time down the stairs, and loaded them all into the truck. The oldest man handed Brian a clipboard, which Brian examined, scribbled on, and handed back to him. And so, the contents of their apartment disappeared down the road.

The apartment now stood stripped, like someone stepping out of a bath—except with no towel in the offing. Yet, Rondo could not remember Brian and Ginny smiling so broadly. They were beaming—Ginny in an earth-tone tunic over blue jeans with a simple braid in her hair and Brian in a short-sleeve velour shirt over Sansa-belt slacks. Ginny took two keys out of her purse and handed them to Brian. Brian took a ring of keys out of his pocket and removed two of them. He dropped the four keys into a drawer in the kitchen and closed the drawer with a solid bang.

"Ready?"

"Ready!"

Ginny held out Rondo's jacket—the one with the baseball patches for the Sox, Brewers, and Yanks. The three put on their coats. Ginny handed Rondo a small suitcase and picked up a larger one herself. Brian picked up yet a larger one. They left the apartment for the last time.

Moments later, they were getting into the relic. That's what Ginny called their tired green Studebaker sedan with the white top. According to Ginny, the car was old enough to have its own children. "It's a damn good car and well maintained," Brian always said in its defense, to which Ginny always responded, "It's all we can afford right now. I know." They rattled down the street past the Black Stallion. Rondo saw a shadow leaning against the usual corner. Two eyes seemed to follow them as they drove past. Stretched across the shelf above the back seat, Rondo looked out the rear window of the car and watched the shadow grow smaller and smaller.

As their car picked up speed, Brian turned up the radio. Ginny turned it back down and spoke as if to the ceiling for Rondo's sake, "Ronny, I didn't tell you earlier because I didn't want you to worry about it. But we're moving."

"We're moving what? Where? What?"

"Your father got a new job—a very nice job—in a lovely town—a very nice town that you'll like very much."

"What?"

"We'll get there in a couple hours." Ginny beamed back at Rondo perched on the rear shelf.

"Where?"

"You'll see." She turned around and settled into the sedan's front bench seat. "You're going to love it."

"You're not pullin' a fast one on me, are ya?"

"When have I ever pulled a fast one on ya?" Ginny smiled. Reaching into her pocketbook, she pulled out a stick of chewing gum. "Fruit Stripe?"

Rondo rolled off the shelf, plunging onto the seat below, and then bounced up to stand on the carpeted hump over the drive shaft, leaning his head and shoulders over the back of the front seat between his father and mother. "Yeah-yeah-yeah!" He grabbed the stick of gum from Ginny and dropped down behind the seat. In a moment he reappeared, chewing, again leaning arms and head over into the front seat.

Looking forward through the windshield, Ginny held out an open hand in front of Rondo. He placed a wadded-up wrapper in her open hand, which she placed in the ashtray in the armrest of the car door.

Peering ahead at the traffic, his attention was drawn to a big green sign. "What's that say?"

Ginny began to read out loud, "The first word is 'Narra-gansett'."

"That's that ale XXX."

Brian broke in, "It's the next town along this highway, and there happens to be a beer named after it, yes."

"The second line says, 'Westerly, Rhode Island'."

Again, Brian broke in to explain, "That's the last town on this highway in the state of Rho Dilan."

"And the third line says, 'New York, New York'." Ginny looked over at Rondo. His jaw dropped and a look of wonder came over his face.

"New Yawk?"

"The town so nice they named it twice," Brian said with false familiarity.

Rondo spoke in worshipful hushed tones, "We're goin' to New Yawk?!"

Trying to answer without breaking his revery, Ginny inclined her head and said in a low voice, "No, dear, we're going to Hartford."

"Well," Rondo said, cocking his head back as he regained his cool, "What's in Har'f'd?"

Ginny looked up at her husband behind the wheel. "There are some very nice people. And there's a very nice job for your father. And there's a nice house for us to live in." She looked back at Rondo. "That's what." She smiled over at Brian who continued to stare straight ahead.

Rondo gave Ginny a long, squinting stare. "Su-u-ure." Rondo withdrew into the back seat.

A half hour later, Brian called out, "Hey, Rondo, how 'bout this bridge?" Rondo roused himself from the back and resumed his position leaning over into the front seat. "Wow!" The bridge thrust four lanes of traffic skyward and then brought them back down on the opposite shore. Shortly after the bridge, Rondo saw more signs. Two lanes continued straight following signs that included what he recognized as "New York, NY." His father steered toward one lane on the right that broke off, apparently following a smaller sign that Rondo assumed read something like "Hartford, Nowhere, Boresville."

Brian's new job title was Maintenance Manager of Noah Wallace Elementary School. The new job was management primarily in title. As Maintenance Manager of the Noah Wallace School, Brian was responsible when either of his two subordinates failed to show up or when he had trouble scheduling them without overtime hours. With a wink and a nod, it had been strongly implied that Brian should try to manage without having to punch the clock on *every* overtime hour that might be necessary. After all, he was "management." And the nice house was an old Victorian painted lady that had long ago lost her many colors. She now wore a modest uniform consisting of several coats of caked battleship grey. She was now an old grey lady. But the house had plenty of space and its own yard, and it backed right up against the side of the school. And this would be the school where Rondo would be attending first grade.

And it wasn't really Hartford, but a suburb. There was no Black Stallion, but a Congregational Church across the street from the school, Hackett's Five And Dime, and Miss Potter's Primary School for Girls. There was a big playground that he could play on—when there were no school activities. And even then, you wouldn't want to get outnumbered on the playground if some other kids were there. But that old grey lady offered plenty to explore for the first few months—a wrap-around front porch and a small back porch, a big front staircase plus a tight turning back stairway, a creepy basement that Ginny ventured into regularly to do laundry, a spooky attic playroom where no one really wanted to play, separate rooms for breakfast and dinner, and more bedrooms than they had beds.

And then there were the people. There were people all around, but they all seemed to go about their business. None of them seemed aware of the house and its inhabitants. For many weeks, it seemed that Rondo didn't exchange a glance with anyone other than the neighbor's cat which seemed always to watch from behind the diamond-lattice windows that looked out from the neighbor's neatly kept house across the neighbor's tidy driveway and the old grey lady's less neatly kept yard.

Roughly three weeks before Rondo was to start first grade, Rondo looked out from his bedroom window across the yard and noticed a boy—about his own age—coming out of the neatly kept house next door. The cat watched from her usual window as the boy headed down the tidy driveway toward the road. He turned crisply onto the sidewalk toward Rondo's house. "Rondo!" Ginny's voice floated up the stairs. "I just got off the phone with Mrs. Driscoll next door." Rondo watched out the window as the boy walked along the sidewalk, glancing up at the grey house. Ginny continued, "They have a son about your age. He's coming over to introduce himself. Maybe he can show you around."

Rondo took one more look out the window at the boy walking along the sidewalk. He headed downstairs and arrived at the front door. He opened the door just as the boy reached for the doorbell.

With one arm in mid-air, the boy said, "Oh, hello there!" He extended his searching hand. "Wyatt. Wyatt Driscoll. Pleased to meet you." He continued to hold out his hand while holding his head at a slight backward angle, taking the measure of Rondo. He looked familiar—like the guy in *The Way We Were* in the movie section of the newspaper.

Rondo kept his hands in his pants pockets as he studied his neighbor. Ginny walked up behind Rondo and placed her hands on his shoulders. "Rondo, say hello," she said through gritted teeth. She smiled at Wyatt. "Rondo, shake

Wyatt's hand!" Ginny knew from her phone conversation that Wyatt was a year older than Rondo—entering second grade. And as she assumed, the name Driscoll was the same Driscoll that Brian worked for—the superintendent of town schools. "Say hello."

Despite the cool introduction, the two boys became regular co-conspirators for the rest of the summer. Wyatt soon introduced Rondo to Teddy, Rondo's other neighbor. Teddy had a little brother who ran around their living room in a baby bumper. Teddy's mother was interesting. Teddy's father was mysterious—mentioned but never seen.

Wyatt and Teddy showed Rondo around. First, how they snuck into the school after the school day was over and rifled through student's desks. There wasn't much there since school was not in session. Wyatt would pull out an abandoned pencil box or a roughly used eraser. Teddy would peer into a desk and find only a couple textbooks that hadn't been collected at the end of the year. Wyatt and Teddy would beam with impish pride. Rondo thought, 'Small potatoes. Not worth my time.'

On another occasion, Wyatt and Teddy steered Rondo toward Hackett's Five And Dime. "Grab some Ring Pops or Chunkys. But not the raisin ones, OK?." When the three of them had casually gone as deep into the store as the candy counters, Wyatt nodded to Teddy and the two of them grabbed handfuls of candy and dashed for the door. A step behind the other two, Rondo did likewise. A half block later they collapsed in the field behind the Congregational Church. With each petty job that Wyatt pressed them into, Wyatt dropped a notch in Rondo's estimation. It was bush-league, pure bush-league.

One afternoon, approaching dinnertime, Wyatt led the other two around the back of Mrs. Potter's school. Finding a set of French doors propped open, ostensibly for ventilation —the boys peered in. Two girls of twelve or maybe fourteen looked out. "Hi!" The girl closest to the window lurched out toward them. "Aw, they are so cute!" The girls squealed. "I'm Marilyn. She's Kay."

"Hi," responded Rondo and Wyatt in unison. They exchanged glances. Teddy took a step backward.

"You want to come in?"

Rondo nodded yes as Wyatt murmured, "We should be going."

Rondo squeezed in. The other two boys peered in but did not move, watching to see what this bold step would lead to—forbidden fruit or dire consequences?

"Would you like some orange juice, ginger ale?" Marilyn offered. Rondo nodded, "Yeah-yeah," without indicating any clear preference. The other two boys continued to stare, rapt, from the safety of a yew. "We have our own kitchenette. Here, you want a couple Hydrox?" The second girl offered him two cookies and tossled his hair. They heard a knock at the door. The first girl called, "Just a minute!" And then whispering, "Here get behind this curtain. Shhh." Rondo shuffled into the corner of the room as the girl pulled the curtain in front of him. The other two boys ducked out of sight.

As the door from the hallway opened into the girls' suite, a new voice entered, an older authoritative female voice. From his post behind the curtain, Rondo could see the faces of the two boys crouching outside the window—eyes growing big with fear. "Miss Wiggins reported some urchins scuttering around the back of the school. She was afraid there might be shenanigans afoot."

"Not here, Mrs. Sutherland. We haven't seen anything."

"Nope, haven't seen anything. No little boys. Nothing like that. Nope," said Kay. "Nothing."

Mrs. Sutherland moved into the room glancing askance at Kay. "Why doesn't that make me feel any better?" She peered out the French doors looking around the building and grounds. Spotting Wyatt and Teddy, she exclaimed, "There, you! Get out of here! Go! Go on!" She waved her hand in their general direction and then paused, waiting for some result of her admonitions. The urchins scampered. Satisfied, Mrs. Sutherland moved back toward the door. "Girls, I know it's been warm these first few weeks, but you be sure to lock your doors and windows. Can't be too careful." As she retreated and the door closed behind her, the two girls stifled laughter. The first girl pulled back the curtain, revealing Rondo, his face full of Hydrox crumbs. Several minutes later, Rondo exited through the French doors and ran as fast as he could back toward the old grey lady. But now he had the clear measure of Wyatt Driscoll.

The school year started the following Monday and things got busy. Lots of standing in lines. Passing stacks of papers up and down aisles. Stand up. Line up. Sit down. Go here. Go there. Line up for lunch. Line up for recess. And recess! How dumb is that. It's the part of the school day when you don't do school. It's un-school. You go to school and your favorite part of the day ends up being un-school, recess, when you act like you're not in school.

But *after* school, sneaking into classrooms took on new danger and new meaning now that the school year had begun. The boys would find a wealth of school supplies and personal sundries in every desk, and Rondo could now connect some of the names with faces like Molly and Leonard and Maxwell. These kids and their teachers had no idea that their stuff was being touched and tampered with—licked, loogied, or stepped on—by Wyatt and Teddy and Rondo. But this was still small potatoes. Rondo itched for something more—to be in control—a boss or at least an earner.

Then about a month into the school year, opportunity came knocking—or ringing. Mrs. Driscoll called to ask Ginny if she could feed their cat. Their great aunt had passed and they would be attending her funeral in Augusta, Maine. Ginny said, "Of course." The next morning the Driscolls were gone.

That afternoon, Ginny invited Rondo to go with her to feed the Driscoll's cat. Rondo followed Ginny over to the Driscoll's back door. He watched Ginny retrieve a housekey from under the doormat. Together they went in to feed the cat. The cat food was on the counter in plain sight. They filled his food bowl and water bowl. The cat slowly jumped down from the perch on the window seat, ate, and returned slowly to the window seat. He looked out the window and then stared back at Ginny and Rondo as if to say, "Are you still here?"

Once in the Driscoll house, Rondo was astounded by some of the treasures they had left behind. Unattended. Unprotected. As if asking to be taken—an AM/FM portable radio, a clock with the two hanging things, a painting of the back of a naked lady—quality stuff.

Monday, after feeding the cat with Ginny and returning to the grey lady, Rondo skulked back to the Driscolls back door, obscured as it was by bushes and large over-reaching pine boughs. Rondo felt for the key, and finding it, tried it in the doorknob. To his astonishment he heard the tumblers fall. Having determined that the cat was a lazy uninterested sort, Rondo felt safe to move about the house. He took a box of pecan sandies. Outside, he found a space between the yew bush and the hydrangeas where the bushes provided a convenient canopy with trunks tall enough to allow a six-year-old to sit and leafy branches long enough to provide cover all around. Rondo left the box under the hydrangea against the fence.

Tuesday, Ginny and Rondo again went to feed the lazy, uninterested cat. This time Rondo watched closely as Ginny approached the back door. Ginny reached for the key, inserted it in the lock, and put it back under the mat. They entered the house. Rondo's blood was racing. Ginny never noticed the missing box of cookies. They served the cat food and fresh water, and they left.

Once back at the old grey lady, Ginny got busy with other things, and Rondo skulked off toward the Driscoll's back door. Once again he entered. This time he disregarded the cat which sat in its usual place and inscrutably scrutinized. He walked softly around the kitchen looking at every shelf and cannister, opening every cabinet, and finally opening the refrigerator. Scanning the room, he decided on a box of saltines and a bottle of shrimp cocktail. Holding the shrimp cocktail in his hand and cradling the box of saltines in the same arm, he managed to navigate the door. He carried them over and laid them down between the bushes against the fence. Standing up, he looked around. No witnesses. He looked back. No sign to tip off a casual passerby to the presence of his stash. He calculated how much more he could store there against the fence, and having made his calculations he returned to the house to continue his work. He removed a glass cannister of multi-color pasta and then returned to take a box of Quisp. He carried out a bottle of cooking sherry that he assumed to be of great value and then in his next trip took Mr. Driscoll's bottle of twelve-year-old Scotch. Setting them against the fence, he admired his handiwork and contemplated what he needed to make his cozy stockpile complete. He returned to work and this time brought out a large jar of dill pickles. On his next trip he grabbed a jar of spiced peaches and threw on top a set of linen napkins. Somewhere on the way back to the bushes, Rondo took something for granted. The spiced peaches escaped his grasp and shattered on the driveway.

Back in the grey lady's kitchen, Ginny heard the sound of glass shattering. She set out in the direction of the sound and arrived at the Driscoll's back door where she found Rondo bent over with a dustpan and a straw broom trying to corral shards of glass and slippery slices of peach.

"Rondo!" She snapped. "What on earth are you doing?"

Rondo stood up straight and gave Ginny a long look. "Mommy." He shook his head. "Don't ever ask me about my business."

Ginny looked down to stifle a laugh and then looked up with a tilt to her head.

Rondo felt like something that was normally in his throat had suddenly fallen to his feet. "Rondo Brian Dunleavy, I will most certainly ask you about your business any time I want to." She took several steps closer. "What are you doing with the broom and dustpan? Did you break that jar?"

Rondo stood, his mouth open, unable to form words.

"And where did you get those? From the Driscoll's house? You went into the Driscoll's house when you weren't supposed to?"

Still no words. His mouth hung open, only his eyes moved—from the Driscoll's back door to the spilt peaches to the stockpile against the fence.

Ginny followed his eyes. Crouching down, she peered into the bushes. "Whu-whu-what?" And then, not wanting to attract attention, she lowered her voice and leaned forward to address Rondo. "Young man, did you take all of this from the Driscoll's house? Did you? Did you!?"

Still Rondo's mouth failed to move. His feet did not move. But the rest of his body was trying to make its getaway.

"Are you going to tell me this all just fell off a truck?" She stood up straight, took a deep breath, and looking skyward she smiled wryly to herself. Composed, she surveyed the scene and looked back down at Rondo. "Life isn't about just taking what you want. It's about making the lives around you better. That's what your daddy did when he brought us here. That's the kind of man your daddy and I want *you* to be." Looking down at the broken jar and spilt peaches, she said under her breath, "That's the kind of man *you* should want to be."

Leaning forward again and looking into Rondo's eyes, she said softly but firmly, "Here's what you're going to do. First, give me that broom and dustpan. I don't want you cutting yourself on broken glass. But you are going to take every single thing you took from that house and you will put it right back where you got it from. Do you hear me?"

"M-m-m."

"Do you hear me!"

"Yes, Mommy." Rondo finally breathed out as if shedding a grave burden. His next breath came calm and peaceful. Something had freed him. He could move his feet again. And as he retrieved the jar of pickles, hugging it to his chest, he recognized a strong, kind woman with a broom and dustpan bending down to gather up his spilt peaches and scattered shards.

Spitfire

Last night the dog days officially arrived: the oscillating fan made its appearance on the dinner table. Every summer, we get a week or two, usually in August, with hundred-degree temperatures and hundred-percent humidity—our mother calls them the dog days. The days are oppressive, and the nights aren't much better. Under these extreme conditions, the normal trappings of civilization start to break down. We start to break down. We start behaving in ways that violate everything we claim to believe in. The heat strips us to our essence and saps our energy and our appetites. Otherwise, I don't think cannibalism would be out of the question.

Last night, when my father got home from work, he wore a glazed expression. Without saying a word or making eye contact, he took off his tie, hung it on the doorknob, and just kept going. He stripped down to the barest civilities, like some boxer entering the ring – sleeveless tee, Bermuda shorts, black dress socks, and patent-leather slippers. Mom, my sister Deb, and I stood in silence and watched as he emerged from my parents' bedroom, walked down the hallway, and descended into the basement. Through the open basement door, we heard sounds of heavy objects being dragged from one side of the basement to the other, boxes being opened and closed, light chains being pulled repeatedly. And then all sounds stopped. A moment later, he reappeared carrying the oscillating fan with the solemnity of a rabbi carrying the Torah.

The oscillating fan is older than I am, with styling out of the '50s and solid steel construction. It harkens back to a time when obsolescence was a failure rather than an objective. This thing was made for the ages. It stands on the table at once hideous and holy, regarded with a mixture of reverence and loathing. We always called it "the oscillating fan" to distinguish it from the box fan, which usually sat in the living room where the consensus (another word for my father) thought it could serve the highest common good. It, too, was all-metal, with less stylistic flair than the oscillating fan. And I think I have the edge over it in years.

About the time that my father loses all concern for respectability or even human society, my mother becomes a broken record. In her defense, she is usually normal. She generally carries on conversations with people and often quite pleasantly. But when the heat starts to get to her, she starts just talking—to no one. Like a cricket, if she's sitting still, she'll sit quietly, with a lot of sighing. But if she gets up —say to get some ice water or a snack or just to look out the window—it starts, and it repeats, and it makes no sense. Last year my sister, Deb, set some of her babbling to the tune of The Banana Boat Song and performed the whole thing bouncing up and down in the shallow end of the Berger's pool:

Boy-O! Bo-o-o-oy-O!
Dog days come an' I wan' 'em to go.
Boy-O! Bo-o-o-oy-O!
Dog days come an' I wan' 'em to go.
It's not the heat, it's the humidity.
Dog days come an' I wan' 'em to go.
Weather not fit for humanity.
Dog days come an' I wan' 'em to go.
'Ey Mister Weatherman, send a couple rain clouds.
Dog days come an' I wan' 'em to go.
'Ey Mister Weatherman, send a couple rain clouds.
Dog days come an' I wan' 'em to go.
Ninety-five, ninety-six, ninety-seven—ugh!
Dog days come an' I wan' 'em to go.
Ninety-five, ninety-six, ninety-seven—ugh!
Dog days come an' I wan' 'em to go.

She nailed it.

With little relief to be had in the house, my parents were up past midnight playing rummy and solitaire at the dinner table in the yellow incandescent light of the fake-candle chandelier. Any game that didn't require speaking to another human being. In our house, the kitchen and dining room are one and the same, but for the sake of decorum, they're separated by a three-foot-high half-wall. Most days, the fluorescent kitchen lights flood the dining room. But on these dog-day summer evenings, we're always careful to turn off the kitchen lights, as if someone (my father) thought they contributed to the heat, but no one had the energy to argue about it. This left the table and those in its miserable orbit cast in a saffron glow, like something that could fit right into Hopper's "Nighthawks." The heat, even at night, drives the unceasing sound of crickets and tree frogs to a pitch that gets on everyone's last nerve. Moths and crane flies attracted by the yellow light buzz around the window screens and the screen door, and then, when you're not expecting it, a June bug will hit one of the screens really hard —Bang! – like a shot from a .22. Your last nerve, boy-o.

Last night, my sister sat in for a couple hands of rummy before dragging herself off to bed. I'd taken my pillow and poured myself out on the floor right in front of the box fan, which my father had positioned in the doorway to the living room in hopes of moving the thick, stagnant air the length of the house straight through the front hall, kitchen, and into the dining room.

Unlike the oscillating fan, which only appeared for a week or two each summer, the box fan usually came up from the basement around the first of July and hung around through mid-September. The all-steel box fan moved a lot of air and made a lot of noise. Sitting close to it came at the cost of not being able to hear anything going on in the rest of the house—conversation, television, stereo, anything. That trade-off was fine with me. I was usually reading a library book or flipping through the Sears catalog or pounding a baseball into my mitt while I listened to the Sox game on a transistor radio with a single earphone.

And morning brought little improvement. We were all dragging after getting fitful sleep and little of it. And we came to breakfast with poor appetites and worse attitudes. Leaning against the kitchen sink, my mother stared blankly out the window and said to no one, "Hey, Mister weatherman, bring us some storm clouds." I looked from my mother, still staring out the window, to my father, in shirt and tie, with his head in his newspaper.

He was seated at the far end of the table, his chair turned to the side as he stubbornly tried to read the morning edition of the Telegraph. He held the paper up in front of his face and shook the pages to full attention each time the breeze from the fan passed over it. With almost every pass of the fan, he would mutter one of his patented exclamations. "Go slammit!" It would be another four or five years before I would realize that "for cryin' out loud," "shiitake souvlaki," "mudger-fudgin'," and "Codnesset" were not quaint exclamations in use elsewhere in the known world, but thinly disguised versions of the juiciest bombs used by everyone else's dads. "Pizza ship!"

We were all in the same house, but we were each in our own worlds. I had come to the table with my Revell one-thirty-second scale model Supermarine Spitfire—an eight-inch version of the plane that had won the Battle of Britain. With a propeller that moved freely and the appropriate camouflage pattern and authentic service markings of the period, the plane banked through the oscillating simulated hurricane-force winds as I held it up to the moving grill of the fan. I sat on the side of the table close to the fan. That way I caught the breeze at the end of its travel. The way the gears worked, it seemed to pause an extra beat or two before it started back in the other direction. And, of course, it was great to get the full effect of the breeze from sitting so close. As the fan started back toward the other side of the table, I moved the plane out as far as my arm could reach, the prop positioned to get every bit of airflow possible. ("K-r-r-rap on a cracker!") And then I'd just sit there watching, waiting motionless for the table-top tempest to turn back on us, as it traveled to the far reaches of the room and then teased its way back again. ("Shut the front door!") And the cycle would repeat. I'd hold her out toward the middle of the table. Then her prop would start to catch the breeze, increasing to top speed as I pulled it back toward me. I'd lead her through a graceful banked turn, and then follow the fan out again with my elegant Spitfire – until its prop slowed and eventually stopped ("Sun of a biscuit!") and I was left longing once again for its tantalizing return, waiting, wilting.

My mother brought toast with concord grape jelly and deposited it on the table. No one looked at it. No one touched it. ("Boy-O boy, it's gonna be a hot one!") No one was cooking this morning. And no one really wanted much to eat, especially anything hot. ("It's not the heat, it's the humidity.") ("Shut the fu-ront door!")

My sister Deb appeared in the living room. She turned on the Today Show and then planted herself on the sofa, pulling her feet up beneath her. I had no appetite for jellied toast or conversation. ("It really is the humidity. But it's the heat, too.") I got up from the table and went into the living room to resume my position from the night before.

Now encapsulated by the roaring slipstream of the box fan, I turned my attention to the airflow over the wing surfaces of my illustrious Spitfire. The aeronautics and sleek design seemed sufficient, even in a scale model, to achieve lift, the plane rising from my hand—or maybe I imagined it.

The Spitfire, so named for its Eight. Thirty. Caliber. Browning. Machine guns. Opposing pilots quake at the sight!

But what that name came to mean to the people of Britain—and anyone who flew one or fought one or simply saw one up close—was the graceful contours of its unique elliptical wing. The compound curves that flow from the nose through the wing to the tail. Reduced drag and increased speed up to Three. Hundred. Seventy. Eight. MPH.

I imagined my airship maneuvering in and out of towering cloud banks to avoid German fighters; and climbing and turning out of the sun to spring furious attacks on unsuspecting bomber formations. The voice of Winston Churchill provided the voiceover: "We shall fight on the beaches, we shall fight on the landing grounds, we shall fight in the fields and in the streets . . . I have nothing to offer but blood, toil, tears, and sweat!" He waved his top hat with one hand and stabbed the other fist into the air. "It's beastly already, this heat and humidity," as he placed his top hat back on his head and clamped down on his cigar with his bulldog jaw. Ultimately, as the sun set over a free Britain on the final day of October 1940, Hitler had lost his stomach for air combat over Britain—thanks to the Supermarine Spitfire and the brave men who flew them!

As my father prepared to leave for work and my mother settled down at the table with a cup of iced tea and some magazine or other, I parked my plane on the coffee table and headed out to the garage where my bike beckoned. Even during the dog days, a kid could escape on a bike—escape from the heat, from society, from whatever ails him.

For her birthday, my sister had been given a glorious 3-speed 26-inch Schwinn Traveler with dual hand brakes and pink-and-white handlebar streamers. Then, without any prompting, in an impressive show of sleight of hand and misdirection, my father assembled the best parts available from the household's other bikes and basically gave me my sister's old bike—a single-speed 20-inch coaster-brake bike with a banana seat and raised handlebars. It could pass as pretty cool, with one glaring exception: The bike had a girls' frame—no ball-buster bar. The old-style girl's frame had two s-curve riser bars connecting the seat tube to the steering tube. I give my old man credit for good intentions but bad follow-through. My sister's old bike, the source of the frame in what's now my bike, had come with an additional bar that could be installed between the top of the seat tube and where the uppermost s-curve met the steering tube. It vaguely resembled the external gas tank from a P-51 Mustang. When he'd originally announced his plans, he'd left the bar on the kitchen table, a visible promise to deliver on his plan. My mother had promptly moved it to the bookcase by the garage door as soon as his back was turned. From there it'd made its way into the garage where it sat for a couple of weeks on the workbench. And then my father eventually moved it to the storage shelves on the far side of the garage, where it continues to sit today. I had basically been sentenced to a summer of riding a girl's bike. To make matters worse, Mark Robbins [right next door] won – won —a new Raleigh Chopper at the July Fourth Lions Club Picnic Raffle. I must admit it was glorious: a sixteen-inch front wheel, a twenty-four-inch rear wheel with a racing-slick tire, high-rise handlebars, banana seat with a back rest, dual handbrakes, and a 5-speed gear-shifter mounted on the top bar. The visual effect was that of the Zebra Three Gran Torino from "Starsky and Hutch." Meanwhile, I was riding the equivalent of a beat up Chevy Chevette.

But this week there's no Mark Robbins [next store] on his dreamy new chopper. The Robbins are on vacation. Pony League is over for the summer. ("We was robbed!") And every year the Robbins go on vacation right after the regular season ends. They go somewhere in Maine, some campground on the fringes of civilization where all they do is canoe and play ping-pong and put nickels in a jukebox. No payphones, no toaster ovens. The Dunlops are gone, too. Gone to see their grandfolks in New Hampshire. That means I'm left with no one my age except Bernie Rochefort —or just Roach, or, if you prefer, Roach-face, Roach-fanny, Roach-fart, or any other combination of "roach" with any word beginning with "f". (Yeah—that's the best one.) We pick on him not just because his name is easy to make fun of, but he also has a weird mouth. His lips are constantly puckered. They seemed always to show his front teeth. And then when he actually smiles, he looks like one of those Scandinavian cloth dolls with the painted elf faces. Roach is normally fourth or fifth on my list of kids I want to hang out with in the neighborhood, but this week, it's him and me. I can only play the hand I've been dealt.

Still, as a kid on a bike—even a girl's bike—this summer has been marked by reaching new destinations. For three or four years, now, we've been able to bike as far as the dairy bar (five cents for one scoop, a dime for two, fifteen cents for three) or the Cumberland Farms in Ware Center. This spring we spent a lot of time exploring our road, Greenwich Plains Rd., in the other direction—past the horse pasture, past the farm with the goon on the front porch, past that blue house, and as far as the gravel pit at the intersection with Cummings Road. Then, right after school let out, five of us followed our road all the way to where it runs into the reservoir. That was a cool ride, but there's always teenagers hanging out at the reservoir, so no thanks. The road by the horse pasture is a great straight strip—perfect for racing bikes. Then the road takes a turn and you hit a little rise that takes the wind out of your sails. Then a little downhill stretch follows as you go past the Krols' farmhouse where the retard sits. And then you hit the biggest hill on the street. So, you have to get over that rise and then get back up to speed as fast as you can to have a chance to make it all the way up that hill without getting off your bike. But you've got plenty of incentive. That derp is usually sitting there on the porch staring out at the road with his tongue hanging out. My mother says he's "touched by God" and then laughs. She calls him a full halfwit. Just simple from birth, she says. But you wouldn't want him to come after you. My father says he prolly has super-human strength—common in the case of mental defectives. They say they took him to the state hospital and came right back with him. They wouldn't take him. Probably too dangerous.

So, for today, I figure I've got three options: One – just lie around the house. The hell with that. Two – grab my army-surplus web belt and fill up my Scout canteen and explore Cummings Road on my bike. If I make it to the end of Cummings, I can get to Doanes Road and then come out at Ware Center and complete a loop, about a twelve-mile ride. That would be something new. Or three—see if Roach can come out. Maybe he's up for exploring down Cummings Road and Doanes Road. Or maybe four – get my belt, fill my canteen with ice water, swing by Roach's, see if he wants to come along. If so, fine. If not, the hell with him.

So, I headed over to Roach's—it's just three doors down. I get off my bike, drop the kickstand, and walk up to the door. I have to knock pretty hard because they have a sun porch. And they're weird about people entering their sun porch to knock on the inside door. So, you have to knock really hard. I'm about to knock harder, when I see Roach's mom coming through their living room to the door. It's not good when a kid's parents come to the door. Sometimes it means they're doing chores or grounded or not wanting to go outside. And sometimes it just means you'll have to talk to a grownup. "Good morning, Missus Rochefort. Can Bernard come out?"

"Let me see." She turns and sings soprano, "Bernard, your little friend's here." Turning back to me, she says, "Just a minute." She closes the door and goes back into the house. I can see her heading back through their living room and meeting Bernie as he reaches the bottom of the stairs. I can't hear what's being said, but his face falls and he shakes his head in resignation. His mother continues up the stairs.

Bernie comes to the door and sticks his head out. "Hi, Jack. I'll be right out, but my mother says I have to bring my cousin along." Without further explanation, he disappears into the house again and I can see a pair of tan legs descending the stairs. They're attached to a pair of navy-blue shorts and a green floral top. The face that was attached was more normal—not like Bernie's. The eyes were smiley but in a more pleasing way. As she crosses the porch, I can see she's maybe an inch or two taller than me. She still has a boyish figure, but there is definitely a hint of some styling, some compound curves that remind me of something and at the same time seem like something altogether new.

"Hi." I played it cool. I might have to find a way to free myself from this situation. "You're Bernie's cousin?"

"Yup."

I turned to Bernie. "You never mentioned having any cousins?"

"I don't have to tell you everything, Jack." Bernie seemed to be trying to look like he was in charge in front of his cousin. Bernie's never been in charge in his life.

"Where you from?"

"Woostuh."

"Gee, sorry to hear that."

"Oh. You're from someplace better? Or do you just live . . . here?" She delivered the line with a pained smile and a squint. Well played. Roach had never mentioned cousins. That meant either he didn't want anyone to know about them or they didn't want anyone to know about him. She actually seemed . . . pretty cool.

I ignored her barb and redirected at Bernie,

"Maybe you should introduce us. That might be a nice thing to do." I gave him an exaggerated head nod. I turned to his cousin, "I'm Jack."

"Claudette." She tilted her head slightly as she said it.

"Claudette?" I smiled. "What do people call you? They don't call you 'Claudette' every time they talk to you, do they?"

"We call her 'Claudzilla' most of the time!" Bernie interjected, stepping forward slightly. He was clearly trying to establish his position in this new group.

She shot him a look like she was cracking a whip. "Bernie, no one calls me that," she said holding up her fist, "and lives!" Turning back to me, she replied in a normal tone, "I go by Etta."

"Who calls you 'Etta'?" Bernie blurted out, as if it was pulled out of thin air. "No one calls you Etta!"

"My friends at school, that's who!" Again, she turned from an angry look directed at Bernie to a more pleasant attitude toward me. Then she glanced quickly back at Bernie, "Kids in sixth grade are a lot more grown up than fifth-graders." Her eyes widened to emphasize "lot" and she almost spit out "fifth".

"Yeah, Bernie." I piled on just for the fun of dissing on the Roach—and just in case Etta thought I might be a sixth grader.

Bernie tried to ignore my cut altogether. "You know," he turned to look at his cousin. "Etta's family lived here like six-seven years ago—up around Cummings Road."

"Really? I was thinking of maybe exploring up that way."

"Tha'd be cool!" she blurted out. "We could go by my old house . . ." She seemed to catch herself. Too much enthusiasm. She continued in a more casual, measured tone. "Bernie says I've developed a Woostuh accent," she continued, "but you should hear our landlady tock. She's like eighty yeahs oold and she tocks wickid fast. She dun't say 'Woostuh' like normal people. She says, 'Wista.' She talks really, really fast."

"Yeah, Wooster's, what, less than forty miles away?" I followed up. "But people there talk like they're from another planet. As bad as Boston – worse than Boston!"

"Yeah. Everyone should talk like theyuh from Wayuh. Right." She looked away dismissively. I turned toward Bernie, but I watched her from the corner of my eye. Looking at Bernie, she continued, "So, we're riding bikes?"

I turned to Bernie, "Does she have a bike? Do you have a bike she can ride?"

Bernie looked at me. "No-o-o-o." He gave me the long No, like it was obvious. "But you can sit two on your bike, right?"

I looked back and forth between the two of them. "Ye-e-ah. But I may not be able to make it up the big hill past the farm with someone else behind me."

Etta jumped in, "So we'll walk up the hill." She looked from me to Bernie. "That's the Krol farm, right? They're my cousins. Our name's Krol, too."

I turned again to Bernie. "So, you're related to the Krols! You never mentioned that!"

"Well, it never really came up." Bernie was on the defensive big-time. "They're like second cousins to me, like hardly related."

"Well, let's get going, then." I looked at Bernie and then turned my bike to face down the driveway while Bernie retrieved his bike from the open garage. I looked at Etta, "Hop on."

She rested her hands on my shoulders to steady herself as she stepped over the seat and then moved her hands to grab the seat directly beneath her. "G'head." And we started off, a little unsteady at first, then we smoothed out as we gained speed. Bernie jumped out a little ahead of us. We went down his driveway and then out past our house and a couple more houses and then we were into the straight stretch by the horse pasture. I built up speed on the long straightaway. My thoughts returned to soaring through the skies over England. We'd been scrambled: radar picked up bombers headed for London. RAF fighter squadron four-one takes to the skies. Unconsciously, I had begun growling like my Rolls Royce twelve-cylinder Merlin engine: "R-r-r-r-r-r!

"What you say?"

"Oh—I was pretending like I'm flying a fighter over London during the Battle of Britain."

Etta said nothing for a moment. "Ok, be a dawk."

I said nothing for a moment. "R-r-r-r-r-r." I'm pedaling hard, picking up speed as we approached the rise before the farmhouse. We actually made it over fairly easily. And then as we started downhill I saw the goon sitting on the porch. He was sitting there like he always does, in his overalls, staring toward the road with his tongue hanging out.

But then he sits up, like he recognizes us. He seems excited. He gets up from the sofa. He's freaking me out. He's like six feet tall. If he comes after us—but I'm catching a little extra speed after that rise and pedaling hard. We're going to clear this hill and leave him behind.

As I started to really attack the hill, I had to stand on my pedals. I needed all twelve cylinders of my magnificent liquid-cooled Rolls Royce Merlin engine running at maximum RPMs, cranking out 650 boiler horse power in order to make it. But each pedal stroke was harder than the last. We were losing speed. About halfway up the hill, I felt my center of gravity shifting. Turning back, I saw Etta turning toward the farmhouse and waving. And then we entered a stall. My pedals were now immoveable and time itself stood still. What happened next was over in an instant, but it felt we were joined to eternity. For one moment glory mixed with disaster as my bike's forward progress completely stopped. Me and my bike were both completely motionless for one moment outside of time. And then motion started in retrograde. And accelerated. I could feel we were moving back and to the left. I instinctively reached back with my left arm to try to prevent Etta from falling. I swung my right arm across my body as I tried to break my own fall. And everything got crazy. I ended up hitting Etta in the mouth with my left hand. My hand continued and struck her somewhere on the way to her left shoulder—I think I know where. She then turned with catlike grace and caught herself with her hands and her left foot and executes a perfect roll. I, on the other hand, saw pavement rudely rising to meet me. With my left arm down and my right arm out, I managed a clumsy barrel roll on my left shoulder. I may have hit my head. I ended up lying on the sandy shoulder of the road. I was at least dizzy if not momentarily blacked out. I couldn't be sure. Either way, I was momentarily disoriented. I saw stars and it took me a moment to make sense of staring into the sun and a hazy cloudless sky. I heard the angry sounds of Etta critiquing my piloting skills. And then I saw a hulking shadow moving rapidly into my field of vision—new overalls breathing through an open mouth with his tongue sticking out of the corner of his mouth. He eclipsed the sun and then the eclipsed sun began to crest around his head. Thoughts flashed through my hazy head. Sol Invictus crowned with light? No. And then out of the dark chaos, I saw a peaceful face in overalls leaning down toward me. "Little man, why do you persecute me?" And the face pulled back and became once again the goon with the tongue hanging out the side of his mouth. "Bebe, Bebe! You okay?" the hulk was frantic, yelling. "Bebe. Ando love Bebe!" The hulk was grabbing Etta in a bear hug and picking her up in the air. Still struggling to regain clarity and balance, I sprang to my feet, unsteady, and charged at the overalls to try to free Etta from her attacker. Etta, who had been distracted from her tirade about my piloting, had turned with a smile and joyfully greeted the hulk in overalls. Then she turned back to me. "What're you doin'? Y'idgit! That's my cozzin! Lee malone! Don't tock t'im like he's some tod."

Bernie, who had made the top of the hill easily, had by now circled back and stopped his bike at the crest of the hill. He shouted down toward the group, "Hi, Ando! You guys okay?" Bernie seems to be late for everything.

I stepped back and allowed the two a moment of greeting. After hugging and greeting Etta, Ando turned to me and smiled. He patted me on the head. He shook his head like an Irish setter. Then he smiled. "Nice . . . little man." Ando turned to pick up my bike. He made a show of brushing it off, ineffectually.

"Ando," Etta explained, "we're tryna get up this hill. But dawko, heah, didn't know when to stop and wok."

Ando looked back and forth between the two of us and the bike. "Ando can help." He nodded his head and moved his tongue from one side of his mouth to the other.

"Come on," I started to say, "Let's just walk up and go from there."

Etta gave me a stare. "Be man enough to accept help when it's awffid." We had somehow transcended the dog days.

Ando steadied my bike as I climbed back on and Etta climbed on behind me. As I looked forward up the hill, an unseen force began to move us up, faster, faster, until we seemed to fly over the crest of the hill. But London was not beneath us. I looked back over my shoulder, and I could see Ando smiling, waving. And then, seeming to realize for the first time that he was standing in the road, he ducked his head and ran back toward the house.

We continued our intended trek. We rode in silence until we turned onto Cummings Road. I heard a voice in my ear. "You know, that was a pretty bone-headed move back there, right?"

"Yeah."

"And you know that was all your fault, don't you?"

"Bu-u-ut you turned and . . . "

"Don't you?"

"Yeah."

One by one, Etta moved her hands from clutching the bottom of the seat to holding onto my web belt.

On Cummings Road, we had little shade. The direct sun was sharp, and I was sweating, but together with the motion of the bike, the effect was cooling. Before long we had turned onto Doane's and we were coasting down toward Ware Center. By the time we'd made it through Ware Center and completed the turn toward home, Etta had gone from holding onto my belt to resting her hands on my shoulders and her chin on her left hand. My Spitfire had been talking in my ear the whole trip.

Your Presence Is Required

The card read,

Your Presence Is Required:

The notorious Manfred Blake, after searching the far corners of the globe to gauge the darkest depths of the human soul, returns to Blakemont to host an intimate evening salon of literary interplay on the subject of damnation.

Entry fee will be the reading of 10,000 to 20,000 original words exploring the topic

– unpublished, finished or unfinished, complete pieces or excerpts.

Plenteous wine and spirits will be provided.

9:00 PM, Wednesday, October 31.

Répondez S'il Vous Plait.

Three reasons leapt to mind why I should not for the life of me miss this opportunity: 1) Blake has contacts in the publishing world that I would die for. 2) He's sure to have some notables on his guest list. And 3) it just might be a chance to see the great man of letters and my most obnoxious fellow alumnus of Williams fall flat on his fat acclaimed face. I immediately returned the RSVP in the affirmative, marked the date on my calendar, and set about trying to figure out what I could possibly read for such a night—now less than a week away. And perhaps my main reason for attending was that, in fact, I wasn't sure if I still gave a damn.

Manfred Blake had graduated from Williams College, undergraduate and MFA, with most of a first novel completed and a host of industry contacts and introductions weaseled out of Williams faculty. He was the most ambitious if not the most talented of recent Williams graduates. I remember first meeting him and addressing him as "Manfred." He promptly corrected me, "Blake. The name's Blake." What modern writer would presume to go by the single name Blake? But he was able to find a willing publisher who seemed to like the persona as well as the writing and managed to gin up support for him receiving the Prescott Medal, a major award for a first novel that brought with it some meaningful dollars. The prestige of the award was more than sufficient to justify an advance on a second novel, which of course did not live up to the critical acclaim of the first. And some in the literary community around Stockbridge suspected that four years out of his MFA program, Manfred Blake—Blake—was struggling to create. That's when he took off on his inspiration tour ala John Hammond, seeking out obscure regional folktales and legends in the hopes that he might find inspiration for his next great novel. The running joke had him doing the Robert Johnson and selling his soul to Old Scratch at the crossroads, and, so, his next book was sure to be a *New York Times* Number One bestseller.

Blake lives in the old Pilkington House, an old stone homestead with mansard rooves perched atop the highest point of land overlooking Mohawk Lake in West Stockbridge. The house was built largely of marble ported by the Hudson and Berkshire Railroad, which was created explicitly to convey marble from West Stockbridge to the Hudson River Valley, a task previously performed by teams of oxen. The railway commenced operation in 1838 amid the frenzy of robber barons building Hudson River Valley second homes and "cottages." But once the appetite for marble manses waned, the railroad failed to prosper, as did the stockholders, and it ceased operation in 1854. But while the freight cars and the good times rolled, the President of the railroad, Herbert Pilkington, a man of modest means at the outset of the venture, built one impressive rambling manse. (I learned all about it in my copywriting internship with Bresard Advertising writing the "Events of Local Interest" column for *What? Where?* magazine.)

Prior to Blake buying the house, it had been one of many Hudson valley hilltop mansions waiting to be rescued from neglect and obscurity by some tentacle of New York philanthropy—the crumbs of the Wall Street table, otherwise known as foundations, tax shelters, or spousal vanity projects. Blake managed to buy the place with a creative combination of historical preservation grants and cash on hand along with a whirlwind of smoke and mirrors. Most charity dollars preferred vistas of the Hudson River to views of Mohawk Lake, meaning less competition. And in the town of Stockbridge, in particular, the currency of his name carried some weight. As part of the deal, he managed to snake through the historical preservationist mumbo-jumbo and officially rename the place Blakemont.

Having RSVP-ed, I set to work selecting a passage from one of my many unpublished works—more correctly, unfinished works—or to be honest, false starts. I hoped to find one contiguous passage that I could read through without embarrassing myself. Unfortunately, I have a confirmed lazy streak of solid gold procrastination running through my core, and my self-respect is not sufficiently developed to move me off the idea of showing up with eight thousand words of an unfinished star-crossed lovers trope.

When the thirty-first arrived, I skated through my school-day schedule of seventh and eighth grade composition classes. The students were distracted by Halloween. Even the usually attentive ones were focused on dress up and parties —more so than usual. About a third of the students were wearing costumes in class. Finally, the final bell rang and the last Frankenstein's monster walked stiffly out of my classroom with a low moan.

I stared at a stack of ungraded papers demanding my attention. I couldn't focus. I threw the papers into my valise, wound my way out to the parking lot, and dropped my case into the trunk of my Nissan Sentra. A carful of students drove by behind me. "Yum! Eat brains!" They were all in costume—ghouls and zombies hanging out of car windows. "Mr. Philpot," one of them cried out, "I'm going to steal your so-o-o-oul!" They laughed uproariously. I gave them a nod and a smile and closed my trunk firmly. You can have my soul. I hate my life. I took my one tweed sport coat off the hanger in the back seat.

The evening's events were supposed to start at eight-thirty, so I had hours to spend but I couldn't focus. I had to drive a couple miles out of town in order to reach a restaurant I could afford—basically, the closest McDonald's. I went through the drive-thru and then parked in the back of the parking lot next to the dumpster. I opened my meal, pulled out my manuscript, and settled in to familiarize myself with the passage I'd chosen for the evening. A spot of red appeared on my title page. I looked down just as another drop of ketchup fell from my burger onto my tie. This is my life. I wiped up the blob on my tie with an index finger and then sucked the blob off my finger. I went after the spot on my manuscript and only managed to spread it. I then lifted my tie to my mouth and tried to lick it clean—the best I could do. Did I mention I hate my life?

I contained the damage and settled into reading through my passage. I read it through a second time. This is actually a good passage. I read it through again and again. I really wouldn't change anything. I read it through aloud. I went over a couple lines to get the tempo and phrasing right. I was actually feeling pretty good about it. I was ready. I drained my soda and put the empty cup, fry carton, and burger wrap in the bag along with the used and unused napkins. I needed to stop at my house to change my tie.

I drove back into town, and as I did groups of kids in costumes thronged along the sidewalks. I couldn't stop at my house. I pulled into the CVS parking lot. As I shifted into park, a zombie with an eyeball suspended on a spring spread himself on my windshield and grunted to the amusement of a group of teenagers. I sat watching witches and princesses and werewolves go by until it was well after eight o'clock.

I then drove through town and turned up Mohawk Lake Road and then into the open iron gates framing the entrance to Blakemont. The driveway wound up the side of the hill, and my stomach churned with butterflies, or perhaps moths. When I arrived, there were only a half dozen cars in the circular drive. Landscape lighting from the center of the circle backlit the cars and illuminated the mists rising form the lake and drifting west to east.

Grabbing my manuscript, I folded it lengthwise and slid it into my jacket pocket. I slammed the car door. I felt more than ever like a writer—or a revolutionary. I approached the looming stone edifice. It was a smaller version of the Victorian robber-baron "cottages" that had been built in the 1840s and 1850s in Newport and along the Hudson valley —evoking Italian villas and Provencial chateaux. (Again, *What? Where?*) A semi-circular portico framed by four Corinthian columns echoed the circular drive with its pedestals and Grecian urns. Reaching the front door, I found a paper sign taped to the door—"Come In. Join us in the Smoking Room." I entered and found myself in a large foyer with more marble columns and a grand staircase. Guests had left their overcoats, hats, and umbrellas on settees around the foyer or on the newel post or the stair handrail. To the right, a set of imposing double doors stood closed. To the left, a matching set of doors stood open, emitting the sounds of people, glassware, and mingled conversation. I followed the sounds.

I was about to enter the smoking room when Blake intercepted me in the doorway. I had forgotten what a big man he was, and chances are he'd gotten bigger since last I'd seen him. His manner was business-like at the warmest. On the cold end of the spectrum, he struck me as anxious, even predatory. "Philpot." He said in his stentorian voice. "Glad you could make it." He was speaking to me without looking at me. He lowered his voice a notch. "You're the bait dog. You're going first. You just have to give everyone a chance to get a drink or two in them. Then everyone else will be eager to read, feeling like they couldn't possibly do any worse. So, no pressure. I'll introduce you. Just keep it loose. I'd like to get things going by . . . ten . . . ish. But Trent Bailey's delayed in the city." I think he looked at me for the first time and then only to see if I was duly impressed. And, yes, I was. Trent Bailey was about the biggest name in the Fantasy/Sci-Fi/Horror/Glam-Gore genre at any of the big five publishing houses.

"Wow." Yes, I actually said, *Wow*. I played the suck-up. But it fit at that moment. The fandom was absolutely genuine.

Blake gave me an emotionless stare and slapped me on the shoulder. I looked around the room collecting my thoughts, and when I looked back to where Blake had been standing, he had moved on. Looking around the room, I noticed Grace Oliphant, reigning queen of murder mystery. Her latest book, "Couscous Monkey Blood" had reached number three this week. She seemed to be talking to Bette Gillette? Bev Gillette. I'd seen her do a panel at a writers workshop for the publishing process. (I'm still not published.) She writes gritty. I suppose you'd say, general literary. It seemed she was the only other female in the room. The ladies were standing by the bar or drinks table. I headed that way.

Moving into the room, I could see that it ran the full depth of the building, with floor-to-ceiling windows at the front and back. The drinks table was set up at the front of the room between two sets of double windows. A large central fireplace in the center of one wall was crackling with a modest stack of firewood. Large overstuffed easy chairs and love seats provided seating. There seemed to be a podium set up opposite the fireplace. The room was large, full of large furniture, for large people or at least large egos. The room was equally dark, with lots of mahogany and black walnut everywhere with large tapestries strategically interspersed. Library shelves covered much of the walls, but the shelves were sparsely filled. I thought I detected a hidden door—on the wall facing the fireplace, a section of bookcase that wasn't exactly plumb and square. I sensed it opened into some secret grotto. But that would have to wait.

I needed only to cross to the left of the room to reach the drinks table. I started and was set upon by someone from my right. He had locked onto me like a heat-seeking missile. "Philpot!" His eyes bore into me. It was . . . Professor . . . Tinker. I remembered him from some class I had completely forgotten.

"What are you doing, Philpot." He had the off-putting affectation of speaking questions as declarations. His speech lacked melody, as if that gave him some advantage in conversational competition.

"Blake invited me to—"

Shaking his head, "No, what are you working on. Where are you living, uh, working." Sip. He took small quick sips of his drink. It might have been seltzer. "What, two years ago you graduated."

"Uh-h-h, yes, two years. I'm working, teaching junior-high English right here in West Stockbridge." Saying it out loud and adding in Tinker's presence convinced me that my invitation had been as a filler or convenience to Blake more than anything. It wasn't the first time that the thought had crossed my mind. I felt deflated from my dinner-time flush of self-confidence. But take what opportunities cross your path, I say. Maybe I really came just to find some way to get back at Blake—embarrass him in front of some people who might matter to him.

Sip. He lowered his voice. "I put in a word for you with Blake." Sip. Wink. "Keep at it." He turned and walked away. I thought to myself, this is what it means to be nonplussed.

The path to the drinks table was now clear. The women had moved away. Not that that was an issue. Bev Gillette was ten or fifteen years older. She could easily have been a Williams summer fling for me. Not that I'm the kind that attracts that. And Grace Oliphant could be my mother, not that that ruled her out as a Williams summer fling, either. I fixed myself a Scotch on the rocks—a good literary drink for settling into a comfy chair. And I grabbed a plate with a couple of bacon-wrapped somethings.

Blake's baritone boomed out over the murmuring of the guests, "Everyone, everyone, everyone—Trent Bailey will be here any minute. Let's plan to get the program started shortly after he arrives and gets settled. Say . . . nine-forty-five?" The small crowd started to slowly migrate to the front windows and the door, as if preparing an ambush. The crowd moved as one, like ocean waters enveloping waders' ankles, ignoring me in some hive-minded hive-blinded unity.

As if on cue, we heard the roar of a sporty convertible appearing over the crest of the hill. He parked at the far end of the circular drive as if to ensure a quick escape. His car was silhouetted by the lawn lamps, and the lake mist glowed as it rolled over it from west to east. A shape emerged from the car. As he crossed the yard and the house lights began to illuminate him, he transformed from black phantom to Trent Bailey, bestselling author, dressed in a Portland Pirates ice hockey jersey with baggy cargo shorts. The crowd buzzed and encircled him like Senators around Ceasar as he came into the foyer.

He quickly got his bearings and soon appeared quite comfortable. "Grace! How are you doing? Number three this week on the Times list! That's great!"

Guests rotated toward him and then away. "Bev," she introduced herself. "So nice to finally meet you."

"Yes, Bev. I liked your . . . one about the coal town." He shook hands. "Charming."

"Mister Bailey!" Tinker pushed forward.

"That's me." Bailey shook another hand and smiled into another face. "And you?"

"Yes, of course, I'm Professor Brad Tinker, Williams' Dean of MFA Creative Writing program."

"Wonderful!" Nodding and turning.

As the rest of the crowd cycled through and introduced themselves, I was able to identify the two other guests that I hadn't made out earlier. The short round gentleman in the heather sweater was O'Leary, Malcolm O'Leary. He writes amazing pieces drawing on Gaelic and Icelandic cultures. His last book was a thinly veiled retelling of Beowulf. The last guest was Peter Chavez, who always struck me as weaselly and uncomfortable in his author photos, but he was looking quite like a normal person this evening. That's why I hadn't recognized him. Plus, like most authors, his photos all seem to be ten years out of date, which I'll probably understand when I'm lucky enough to need an author photo.

As I stood by the drink table, the crowd flowed over and around me again, as I bobbed like a cork. Suddenly a hockey jersey turned around in front of me. I was face to face with Trent Bailey. "Who are you?" Trent asked, holding an oatmeal raisin scone over a dessert plate.

"I'm Ray Philpot—Raymond Philpot." I felt like I was smiling. I should have been smiling. I was giddy, lightheaded. "I'm still working on getting my first novel —."

Blake's voice boomed again, "Trent, help yourself to a drink, some edibles. Everyone, let's find our seats and begin." The guests settled like a murder of crows, starting with those who least desired to impress the other guests.

When the fluttering had died down, Blake now stood alone dwarfing the podium. As the background noise in the room subsided, he began, "Now, everyone, everyone, everyone, . . . The bar is stocked, the snack table is likewise filled to ov-er-flow-ing. Help yourselves. Help yourselves. Help yourselves. The caterers will now depart from us, leaving us to our business for the evening." For the first time, I noticed the three or four catering staff dressed in black who now stealthily exited, collecting empty boxes, trays, and crates. "Thank you," he directed at the exiting caterers. "And now, we begin our program for the evening. What we all believe to be of the utmost importance. I have invited a select group of men and women of letters because I know you to be of the highest quality. Artisans who trade in the highest of arts, skills, disciplines. But also practitioners of the highest moral and ethical standards. Investigators of the deepest, darkest facets of humanity." He looked around the room for effect.

"That being said, let me introduce the first reader for the evening: Ray Philpot." The small crowd applauded politely.

I stood up, unfolding my manuscript, anticipating Blake moving away from the podium. As he loitered there in limbo, I realized my intro was continuing.

"Ray is, like me, from the laudable tradition of Williams men of letters. He has been called the most promising entry into the world of literary talents in the last five years—basically since me." Who has said that? Blake bowed to a smattering of applause. "Please make him feel welcome. Please welcome him as warmly as you would me." He clapped, and turned toward me, bowing his head, and almost as an afterthought, began to move away from the podium.

I took my place behind the podium, positioning my papers. "Good evening. I'm going to read you a story approximately ten thousand words," I lied. "I estimate it's a draft or two away from finished, but that was the assignment." The rest of my time at the podium was a blur.

The next thing I remembered was Trent Bailey saying, "I think if you made those two changes, you're home free. I really liked it." He rose from his seat, extending a business card. "Call my editor. I think he'll really like it, too." Wait, did Trent Bailey just say that?

From the far end of the room, Blake's voice boomed, "This isn't a workshop. This is a salon, a literary evening for our deepened appreciation of the human heart—or heartlessness. Trent, you'll have to contain your enthusiasm. We have a long night ahead of us. And now I think you all know Bev Gillette—certainly some of us better than others." Bev smiled slyly at Blake as he enumerated their many connections, coincidences, and common interests. When he finished speaking, he stared and licked his lips. "Bev?"

Blake gave Bev Gillette a two-handed handshake and pulled her close for a kiss on her cheek. The audience squirmed uncomfortably. Those close to the podium could hear Blake whisper, "I remember that dress." But she took the podium and immediately owned the room. She was instantly business-like, sophisticated, lyrical, gritty, enchanting, insanely vulgar, and completely mesmerizing. She read an excerpt from her book-in-progress. Disembodied coal miners swarmed from their mine homes into the streets and game paths and holler crawls in choruses of Scots-English hymns and drinking songs. The children cried out for food, the women for justice, the men for the restoration of their forefathers' reputations. The languages of sin and oppression swirled and fell to the ground. When her voice stopped sounding, there was stunned silence, and all of us felt a little dirty. I was aware of a physical need for more raspberry scones. But otherwise, I felt completely bedded, bruised, and bewildered by her reading. She could have been a courtesan. One listener just said, "Holy —."

Next Blake introduced Tinker, who had clearly been invited as a courtesy. Blake thanked him voluminously for fueling his career—and made a strong point of how much Blake's success has in turn raised the profile of Tinker's program. Tinker then read a poem that prattled on about Persephone and pomegranate seeds and Hades. Hades lustily wiping his mouth. Persephone licking her lips, running her tongue around her lips and sucking Hades' seed from between her teeth. I remember now: the class was "The Classical Poets: Boethius, Catullus, Horace, Lucretius, and Ovid." In the Classics department, it was referred to on the sly as "Bestial, Awful, and Lurid." Most of us in the English department failed to get the joke. Twelve students signed up for it and six dropped it the first week. I think the six that dropped were in English. So, Hades sets his sights on Persephone, his niece, and he entraps her into a litigious marriage based on a technicality when she performs an act not knowing its significance. Ok, that is pretty spot-on with the evening's topic.

Blake offered his guests a few minutes for a break, and then he invited Ms. Oliphant to read. Once again, he made sure to point out how well he knew her, how she had referred him to her literary agent, and how she taught Blake her five pillars of marketable writing. Blake finished by saying how much her fans were clamoring for the last several years for one more Grace Oliphant masterpiece—a cap to her incredible career. She was not a great reader, perhaps declining with age, but her storylines swirled so effortlessly. Guests ooh-ed and ahh-ed. She read a chapter two thirds of the way through the book—when the detective intuits that the primary suspect actually had a virtuous motive for the behavior that at first seemed despicable. And then the chapter ends with a twist that reveals that the primary suspect is down-right sinister! It almost makes me want to buy the book—or at least watch the inevitable movie.

Blake's voice once again called out across the room, "If everyone would like to refill their drinks, grab a snack or two, . . . it's time for me to introduce. Mister. Trent. Bailey." There was a round of applause, and people scrambled to refill their drinks and settle in. But then, as if remembering his script, Blake clung to the podium and recited every connection he shared with Bailey. When it had become clear that Blake had more introduction to make, Bailey had stepped over to the drink table to freshen his drink. As Bailey stood with his back to Blake, Blake blurted out with a note akin to panic, "And I . . . I was the first—you can confirm this—the very first person to review each of Bailey's. Last. Five. Novels. On Goodreads. His last five." Without having to look around the room, you could sense the audience squirming. Blake, let's not be needy.

Taking the podium slowly, Trent Bailey looked around the room. "In light of Professor Tinker's fine contribution, I suggest not eating anything tonight—if it's not too late." There was a tittering of polite if somewhat confused laughter. Bailey then spoke at length. He seemed clearly uncomfortable with the format, spending a good bit of time explaining the bigger context, what came before and what would follow after. The crowd was clearly deferential or simply awed, including me. When he began reading, he read as if sounding out his words phonetically. Despite a very hard-to-follow reading, the guests greeted its completion with a round of applause befitting his publishing contract. As best I could make out, his main character is basically bullied, wishes ill on the bully, and sees his wish realized. He then feels regret and even more magically sees the malign wish undone. He then wrestles with his apparent power and responsibility for good and evil. So, does he still answer to God? Or not?

Blake then returned to the podium. It was now after midnight. People expected this to be a long evening. For some, this was turning into an exceptionally long evening. But such was the intention. Blake announced he would read three passages from his current manuscript—an opening passage, a middle passage, and a closing passage. He began in a smoky, rumbling voice. As Blake plied his themes, it became clear that the story arc was that of a young antihero pursuing the most direct route to advance first himself and only secondly the welfare of others. His goals seem to keep morphing, degenerating as he becomes more focused on achieving.

As the reading wore on, I think it safe to say that each of the guests gradually came to realize that this work was baldly autobiographical.

Blake peered out at the guests as he launched into his third and final passage. "I've traveled by donkey, camel, elephant, and handcart, from Bangkok to Bombay to Babylon to Bucharest. The single story of the greatest import I bring back to you from Tibet."

Through a series of obscure inquiries and obtuse answers, the hero eventually finds himself in a desolate, snowbound high desert in Tibet outside the hut of a former monk cast out of the monastery.

Blake continued, "'Why did they banish you?'

"'Like you, I wanted to know too much. Come and sit.' He invites the traveler in. Without a word, he sets tea, bread, and fresh fruit in front of him.

"'How do you know I want to know too much?'

"'It's written in the lines on your face, in the dirt on your clothes.' He leans toward the young man, 'You're the only kind of visitor I get.' They talk about the roots of knowledge, the price of knowledge, the power of knowledge. Their afternoon wears on. As evening approaches, the winds can be heard howling outside the hut. The monk looks toward the ceiling. He says, 'I'm afraid I have told you too much already. You must go.'

"'It sounds like a blizzard outside. Is this Tibetan hospitality? Your sending me out into a storm?'

"'That's not a storm. That's the voice of the Tireless One, the Tester—the Keeper. You'll see. Once you leave here, he will enclose you and escort you.'

"'It's getting dark.'

"'He will give you those answers you seek—in exchange for that which you little value. He will give you vision in the darkness—because you shun the light.'

"'Why me?'

"'Because you have eaten the fruit.' The monk smiled for the first time and nodded at the food in front of them. The fruit was half eaten. The tea was half emptied. The bread was broken in two. The traveler recognized the unspoken contract of hospitality: A host explicitly offering, 'What's mine is yours. Share my table,' invites the guest to take what he wants, in keeping with the Great Heart. But the guest who assumes, taking without explicit invitation—a thief.

"'But I never ate or drank anything.'"

"'*I*—never ate or drank anything. But it appears *you* have.' The monk smiled. 'Now if I were to accuse you, you would be convicted. If convicted, you would be sentenced. If sentenced, then that sentence would be carried out.' The monk smiled over at the traveler. 'Who can grasp the truth? It is like the wind. Close your hand and you grasp nothing.' He closed his hand and raised his arm toward the door of the hut and then opened his hand. 'Now please go.'

"It was as the monk had said. As the traveler exited the hut, he was enclosed in an eye like that of a hurricane, filled with deathly silence and stillness. He whispered to me the secrets I wanted to know. And he brought me down from the high place to the river valley and across the border into India. There he left me. But before he did, he told me one other thing. He said, 'Your presence is required. Except for one day every year when you will be free to seek for someone —an advocate willing to stand in your place.'

"'But what if I didn't eat the fruit?'

" 'Whiner. Complainer. What proof do you have that you didn't? This time or some other time? Certainly, you have at some point eaten, taken, deceived, or despised. Tell me with a clean conscience about your pure heart, your spotless soul.'

"There was only the sound of the maelstrom.

" 'As I thought.'

" 'And the sentence?'

" 'As I said, your presence is required. Except for your annual day of trial.' "

Sweat had been beading on his forehead, his upper lip, dripping onto his manuscript pages. He'd been holding the pages tightly. The clock struck one. He turned to the last page and read, " 'I'll waive the sentence if even one person feels sympathy for you. If even one heart winces at your fate. If one person cares.' " The group breathed a collective sigh, shifting uncomfortably, rising to refill drinks. The host looked around anxiously. Someone, I think Tinker, muttered at the drink table, "It's just good that his story isn't about *him*."

Blake seemed to step down from the podium like a man denying his own defeat. He tried to keep up the appearance of a successful reading. And you could almost see in his face the tension of wanting to believe—to believe his words would still have the desired power, in at least one listener, as they continued to churn in at least one mind. The writer remained committed to his composition.

Blake appeared to be not only sweating but silently weeping. He grabbed a cocktail napkin from the podium and blotted his cheeks, his forehead, his upper lip.

Leaving the podium, Blake poured himself a double bourbon and returned to his seat at the far end of the room.

The room fell silent except for the low roar of the fire. Only then did he look up to see everyone waiting for him to announce the next speaker. Chavez and O'Leary looked to each other, Chavez seeming to defer. Blake slowly put down his drink next to his chair, rose slowly, and returned to the podium. He seemed to be a smaller man than just moments earlier. He began speaking slowly, "Next on our program will be Peter Chavez." Blake slowly recounted what must have been every word that passed between the two men in the last five years. He seemed to emphasize the significance of every sentiment. And then blotting his face with another cocktail napkin, Blake cleared his throat loudly and announced in a stronger voice, "Take it away, my dear good friend Peter Chavez!" Blake returned to his seat coughing.

Chavez took the podium, eyeing Blake. The clock struck one, two, and Chavez paused to allow the third strike. "Hi. I'm Peter Chavez. Thanks for having me. I'll be reading a passage introducing the heroes of the Chernobyl disaster from my current historical novel in progress, *Fahrenheit 1,742*." He paused once again. The story as he told it begins in 1986 in Chernobyl, Ukraine. After a core meltdown in one of Chernobyl's nuclear reactor chambers, an explosion destroyed one of the four reactors. Several weeks after the explosion, the plant chiefs became seriously worried that radioactive material was traveling in a molten flow towards the huge pool of water under the reactor. If the two came into contact, it would cause a second steam explosion, potentially destroying Chernobyl's three other reactors. Someone needed to go into the pool of radioactive water and drain it —a suicide mission. According to most accounts, two plant workers and one soldier stepped forward to take on the job. Undoubtedly, the plant workers—and most likely the soldier, too—would have known that the basement of the reactor was highly radioactive. Even if they could get the job done quickly, they would still be exposed to lethally high doses of radiation. The Soviet authorities even assured the men that their families would be looked after financially. As Chavez wove the tale, they were three very different men. They came from three very different backgrounds and mindsets. One was supposedly a patriotic and duty-bound soldier following orders wherever they took him. He felt he did not have the right to make a choice. A subordinate to the state. A cog in the wheel. A servant of his people. The second was an older man, widowed, grown children, physically beginning to fail, past his prime and looking only at the dark side of the hill of life with little to look forward to except recognizing more names in the obituary section and seeing more and more of life's wreckage on his downward journey. A true hero. The third was rumored to be "slow," not able to fully comprehend the risks and the challenges. Simply showing up for another day of work, marching blindly ahead. The plant chief pointed and he went gladly, not aware that there was anything unusual about this day or this assignment. Not realizing this assignment was voluntary. Three very different life sentences read at three in the morning. The plant chiefs, however, damn them, and the bureaucrats that oversee them and the oligarchs who manipulate them. The guests were thoughtful, impressed.

From the far end of the room, Blake began a loud slow clap. The others in the room joined in. Guests commented. "Excellent piece." "Thought provoking." "Can't wait for the book to come out."

Blake echoed, "Yes, very thought provoking, inspirational." He got up to refill his glass. He was walking slowly but showing surprising steadiness for the amount of liquor he had imbibed in the course of the evening. He looked like he had aged, his eyes now noticeably bloodshot and sunken.

Some guests were wide awake and alert. Others showed signs of the toll taken by the long night and the free-flowing liquor. Ms. Oliphant was alternately dropping her head and then waking with a start. I was realizing I would have to go in to work in a few short hours. Overall, the mood had been uncomfortable almost from the start of the readings. And yet, there was very much a sense that no one would leave before sunrise.

The chair that O'Leary had been sitting in was empty. He was once again filling his glass and plate. Returning to his chair, he realized he was the only one yet to read. He grudgingly put his food and drink down next to his chair and moved deferentially toward the podium. He looked toward Blake. Blake motioned for him to wait, sit back down. Black once again rose slowly and returned to the podium. "Malcolm O'Leary. What can I say that I haven't said before about Malcolm O'Leary. Mal, you have such a sense of . . . of loyalty . . . to all of your friends."

"I do?" O'Leary chirped from his seat. Guests chuckled.

"I don't doubt that you would take a bullet," Blake paused for effect and scanned the room, "for anyone in this room."

"I would?"

"You," Blake pointed at O'Leary, "You. You are always . . . sacrificially . . . giving to friends and family."

"I am? I think you'll find I give very selfishly. Very selfishly, indeed."

"Oh, Mal," Blake continued, "we're brothers. Family. Soul . . . mates. I have given everything for you and you for me."

"I'm sorry." O'Leary seemed to be trying to keep it light. "I wasn't aware." He eyed his plate.

Blake tilted his head and gave O'Leary a look that could have been interpreted as drunken love or intent to squash like a bug. "Yes, Malcolm O'Leary! You're last but not least! Give us a rousing reading of your special brand of Irish wisdom!" Blake moved slowly away from the podium. O'Leary seemed to avoid getting anywhere near Blake's possible path.

O'Leary settled himself at the podium and nodded toward Blake. "Thank you, Blake for the honor and for the Guinness!" He raised his pint glass to Blake. O'Leary looked down at his papers.

The clock ticked loudly. The fire continued its low roar and crackle like the uneven breathing of some sleeping colossus. Sometime during the evening, someone must have tended the fireplace without being noticed.

O'Leary spoke with a measured pace in a beautiful voice with the slightest lilt. The sound of his voice transported me to a place somehow farther away than Chernobyl. A timeless place beyond work-a-day considerations. He described how Man left to his own devices cannot hope to escape the tricks and traps of the fae, the fairy people, the magical ones. Reach out to shake a hand. Retrieve it only to realize you're manacled. Share my pot of gold? Serve in my fairy palace. The fairy make their own rules. Yes, because they were here first. A fool tries to bargain when he doesn't understand all the rules. Woe to proud Man who treads heavily on the turf of the Fairy King. The Banshee appearing as temptress and with one turn revealing herself to be hag. "Kiss me noo. I ne'er will come agin."

O'Leary stood at the podium looking down at his manuscript. He folded it lengthwise and slid it into his jacket pocket. He looked up at the guests in their various stages of excitement or fatigue. I sipped my Scotch. I felt myself speak, "That's beautiful."

O'Leary smiled down at me. "Thank you, Raymond." I was doubly warmed.

O'Leary looked around the room one more time. He said, "We're honored to have Ms. Oliphant here, but I dare say we also have an elephant in the room." He emphasized the word "elephant" perhaps to make his enunciation clear. His gaze rested on Blake.

"Yes," said Blake.

"Yes, what?" said O'Leary, "You sold your bloomin' soul to the Divil and now you wants it back?" He laughed. "And the people in this room are your best candidates? Have you never touched a heart? Prayed to your God? Are all your hopes in the powers of darkness? Are you betting on finding a bigger fool?"

Blake gathered himself up and stood with glass in hand. "Someone," he said, "someone must see benefit in trading places with me. Someone? Anyone?!"

"Who in their right mind?" exclaimed Bailey. "Who in their right mind would take that bargain off your hands? You'd have to be Chavez's idiot!"

"Or Chavez's damn soldier blindly taking orders," I found myself blurting out, "Or the old man skidding down the dark side of the hill."

"Well, speaking of skidding downhill into obscurity," Blake said slowly, "How 'bout you, Tinker?"

"What!!"

"Did you think you were invited because you could write?" Blake, with his large head, his red bulging eyes, and flaring nostrils, leaned toward Professor Tinker. "You could go out with some literary recognition besides just the *Williams Review* to your credit. Your wife and children would actually be proud of you. Your obituary would be more than one paragraph. Just think about it."

"You're mad." Tinker looked down, unable to meet Blake's maniacal stare.

"Or you, Philpot!" Blake extended his open hand in my direction. "You've been shopping your first novel around how long now? Get it published *instantly*! Enjoy a little *real* money. And then go out on top!"

"No deal."

Blake searched the room. "Bev?"

"What do you think I am? Some Andromeda or Iphigenia?" she responded. "Plus, didn't they have to be spotless virgins? Good luck with that!"

"Maybe that's why I'm here," said Ms. Oliphant in a quiet voice. Her eyes were closed, though apparently she was only resting them. "Still, no deal."

Blake scanned the room one more time. "How 'bout you, Chavez? Wouldn't you like to take a break from your stuffy brand of non-fiction? Enjoy a moment of critical acclaim?"

"It's historical fiction," shot back Chavez. "And No. I mean—never mind. You do have a way with words, don't you, Blake?" He smiled and nodded toward O'Leary still standing at the podium. "I'd rather serve his damn fairy king that take your deal, Blake. No one here has any reason to die for your sins. And I don't think we could satisfy the terms of your bargain even if we wanted to. I'd bet there's more fine print than even you realize."

"Oh, come on! Anyone?" Blake looked around the room, now looking like a raging bull. "Well, how 'bout this: 'Greater love hath no man than this: to lay down one's life for his friends.'" He took several steps, coming around by the fireplace. "Maximilian Kobe, anyone? 'I'll die for that man.'" Blake now stood with his arms down at his sides. "You call yourselves writers! Purusha, the Hindu god who gave his life to create the cosmos? No? And you piddle away your time creating your little worlds!"

"Blake, I think you may have misplayed this," came Trent Bailey's voice across the quiet room. Murmured agreements could be heard. "Here comes the sun, by the way."

Several of us got up and crowded around the south windows. Rosy fingered dawn was reaching for the Berkshires. As sunlight began to touch the mountain tops, points of light began to glow. A slight breeze, a breath, a spirit seemed to move along them, east to west. It gained strength as it approached. As it reached Blakemont, it seemed to take the form of a wave. Just below the sharp line between daylight and shade, in the twilight border, we could see a phalanx of dust devils, and within their vortices there appeared to be arms and legs and an occasional face—grinning, sneering. The treetops in front of the house gloried with first sunlight. We watched the light move down the tree branches and trunks, interacting with the lake mists as it dropped. The twilight dervishes stayed below the level of the sun's rays, momentarily reversing the motion of the mists, frantically churning east to west and then reverting calmly to their usual west-to-east motion as the light hit them, the dervishes gone. Then the sunlight began to pour into the front windows, bathing the bookshelves starting at the top of the room, illuminating the gilded spines of the old editions. Slowly, the light reached into the smoking room.

Staying at the back of the house, Blake seemed to become increasingly uncomfortable. He seemed to sizzle, like a bacon-wrapped something. We turned as one to watch his possible immolation. Bev Gillette was the first to approach him.

"Bev!" Blake called hopefully until he realized she was only drawing nearer to him to see more clearly his insubstantiation.

"What the–?" Bev said peering at Blake. "It's . . . prismatic, not quite translucent."

Grace raised her head and looked over at Blake. Suddenly she was up and walking in his direction, walking around to see him from different angles, like a detective at a murder scene. "How would you describe that? Flickering? Opalescent?" She looked thoughtfully over at Bev Gillette. "Trying to understand the process involved. Hmm."

Still standing by the front windows, Chavez stared coldly at Blake while Tinker shot Blake a sly searching look. Trent Bailey looked out the windows at the advancing rays and the retreating shadows.

As Blake's substance waned his voice seemed to follow, and he could be heard to say, "Maybe next year." And then he blinked out. And in the absence of his physical presence, again, his voice could be heard, weaker, as though only an echo, "Maybe next year."

Trent Bailey, still standing at the drink table, reached for the one unopened fifth of bourbon. He turned to face the crowd and said, "My work here is done." As he walked out the door, I heard him say to himself or anyone who cared to hear, "Boy, I've got this one written already!"

Strange

A deep sense of satisfaction warms me as I park along the curb in front of my townhouse. In the past year, I've refinanced my school loans, and last week I closed on my townhouse on a gentrified block in the Sunnyside neighborhood of Morgantown. I feel . . . at home. And I feel like I am just beginning my life as an adult—a first-generation born-in-America son of Filipino immigrants. Walking up my steps, pulling out my keys—*my* keys to *my* house—I insert the key, turn the knob, and enter. Pulling the door closed behind me, I'm embraced by a peaceful quiet, in *my* space. Dropping my keys on top of one of the piles of boxes by the door, I look over an ocean of similar boxes spread throughout the living room. On the opposite wall I see a single 5x7 photo frame propped on the mantel holding a photo of Rico and Esmerelda, Mr. and Mrs. Esteban—Mom and Pop. He's wearing a blue golf polo slightly stretched around his generous belly with his arm around my mother's plump physique—seven-months pregnant. With their free hands, they hold aloft small American flags on their proudest day—

the day of their naturalization—taking the oath to become American citizens.

I remember I have a living room full of boxes concealing what I have and five other rooms with mismatched pieces of furniture revealing what I don't have. I *do* have a breakfast meeting in the morning two hours away in Charleston. There's a hotel reservation waiting for me if I choose to go tonight—or I can just get up incredibly early tomorrow—I can't; I have to go tonight. There's nothing in the fridge. And I still don't have a shower curtain. I'll pack a suitcase, grab my briefcase, and I'll get something to eat on the road. And if I get to my hotel in Charleston, I can expense my dinner. As quickly as I'm home, I'm just as quickly back on the road—a five-foot-six road warrior with my best suit hanging behind the driver's seat.

I was hoping to get to Charleston before nightfall. I made it about halfway without a hitch, making the most of the precious late-February daylight. I-79 from Morgantown to Charleston cuts almost straight down through the heart of West Virginia, like a knife. The product of modern earthmovers, it follows what prior to construction of the interstate was an imaginary line running through hills where hills had to be removed and through thin air where roadbed had to be built up. But this thin line of the modern is not immune to the primal—especially in winter. A quick snow squall can blow up in the blink of an eye and suddenly drivers can lose visibility—enough for a car to veer off the road. First responders are generally quick to the spot as long as they get a call. Almost on cue, my GPS flashes "Road Closed Ahead—Accident—Delay: 30 minutes" just before it begins to blink intermittently, "No signal." I decide it's a good time to get off the highway and grab something to eat. If it says thirty minutes, it'll probably be an hour. Let the emergency crews clear it up before getting back on the road. I get off at exit 67 and decide to follow 4 south. Going from the open interstate to Route 4, everything seems to close in. The two-lane highway makes me feel claustrophobic after the open interstate. The road follows a winding river as wooded hills fold in and out and dense hardwoods—beech, maple, and cherry—overarch the road and white birch run down to the river. This road—this river path—might be laid right over the same game trails and goat paths used by the first inhabitants of this area. As the river and the road continue to serpentine, I lose any sense of direction. My GPS freezes. Immediately off the interstate, I had passed one eatery —"The Three Lil Pigs BBQ" in neon and underneath a wooden sign saying simply "Diner." I saw that the parking lot was filling up with travelers apparently responding to the same impulse. But I had decided to go on to the next opportunity down the road where I might find less of a dinner rush. As I notice the sky dimming, my GPS switches to night mode, and I switch on my headlights. In the twilight, my lights washed over a tall, thin man with a bushy beard leading two mules along the opposite side of the river, and I begin to second guess my decision. And then my headlights hit a simple, white-washed wooden sign declaring, "TRAdINg POST." I parked on the near side of the small log-cabin-style building. I anticipate a very kitschy version of West Virginia Mountaineer dining and probably a few tables of hillbilly giftables and souvenirs. As I park, I see no other cars in sight. I assume patrons are local or parked on the far side of the building, as amber lights shine out through windows on three sides.

Entering the building I walk up to the bar. The man behind the bar, with the sleeves of his flannel shirt rolled up to his elbows, says, "Welcome to the Trading Post. Whatcha got to trade?" I notice there are no stools along the bar.

I look around. "Me? I'm just looking for a bite to eat."

"Well, we barter with a lot of people 'round here." He smiles. "Keeps the tax man from getting' tween people."

"You mean like I bring you a sack of beans and you give me a hamburger and fries?"

He laughs. "Not 'xactly. Say a feller bags a deer. He takes it to his local meat processor. He tells him to send the meat to me. The meat processor takes his share. No cash changes hands. That feller then has a balance here. He can redeem it in taters or," he looks around the room, spotting the display by the door, "or t-shirts or shot glasses." He turns and points to a small bulletin board next to the door. "Or services. One guy'll do your taxes. We got a guy's a glass blower."

"Can I pay for my meal, then, or do I have to trade you something for it?" I ask.

He smiles. "No, I can cash you out. What can I get you?"

I say, "What's your specialty?"

He looks at me, pausing, and says, "I could whip you up some cornbread. The skillet's hot." He looks toward the back of the room, and turning back, says, "We got some fresh elk and pheasant. Some grouse, rabbit. And I got me a mess of venison stew that I put up yesterday."

"Any veggies?"

"Vege-tables?" he pronounces with an extra syllable. "I got some ramps and taters I could fry up? No maters to speak of. We only get greenhouse-grown this time of year."

You don't spend four years at WVU without learning the quaint food lingo—taters for potatoes, ramps for little green peppery, garlicky onions, Molly Moochers for a certain mushroom with a nutty almost smoky flavor. Maters: tomatoes. I figure I'll be safe going with one of the traditional fast foods of West Virginia culture. "How about some pepperoni rolls?"

"No furrin food." He looks at me deadpan for a moment, and then his face breaks into a broad smile. "Just kidding, but we don't have any at the moment."

"I'll take some fried ramps and taters and a little cornbread." I order with a slight smirk as if sharing the joke with the barkeep. "And how about a Pepsi?"

"I'd rather work out a trade," and he pulls a stoneware jug from below the bar. "But we do have Pepsi." He places a warm can in front of me, and heads down the bar to my right where he begins to labor over a large wood stove with two skillets, a wide-mouthed stew pot, and an old, blackened coffee pot on top. Looking back over his shoulder, he says, "Take a seat. I'll bring 'em over to ya when're ready."

I look around the room. Two other souls sit hunched over plates of food, one facing away from me, and the other sitting along the back wall in the far corner. The man in the corner looks up at me periodically as he eats. The windows now look out on a dark, wooded landscape and out over the winding river. Three long, family-style, wooden tables line the walls on two sides with benches along the wall and several bent-willow chairs on the opposing sides of the tables. I take my jar and maneuver into a seat along the back wall, facing the front of the "trading post."

Shortly, the barkeep brings over a hot plate of steaming potatoes and fried green onions with a generous piece of cornbread. "Salt 'n' pepper's on the bar." He looks down at me momentarily. "You don't have a knife." He seems puzzled. "You need one?"

"Please," I reply. "And a fork would be nice."

His puzzlement seems to intensify. "You ain't got no meat, there. You need a *fork*?" He looks at me, shaking his head. He mutters under his breath, "Kids is soft these days." He walks back behind the bar and searching, pulls out a hunting knife and a straight, two-tined fork. I thought, Really, Daniel Boone? Maybe you're taking this schtick a little too far.

Before the thought clears my mind, the diner who had been facing the wall moves suddenly, dragging his chair over and slamming down his plate across the table from me. "You care for some company?" Without waiting for a response, he returns his attention to his plate and continues eating. "The venison stew is mighty filling." He wags his head and then looks up at me. He strokes his dark, shaggy beard with his thin bony hands. He's wearing something resembling a shearling coat over a simple shirt with a laced placket.

I continue to examine him momentarily. "What town is this?" I fumble with my over-sized utensils, cutting my potatoes and green onions.

"This here's Strange."

"Yeah, I agree." I reply with a smile. "But what *town* is this?"

"This here's Strange." He stares at me. "This here's Strange, West Virginny. They changed its name some years back. They named it after Willum. Willum Strange." He lunges forward, placing one arm on the table. "Somebody found a set of bones sittin' against a tree down along Turkey Crick. Under his hand bone they found a note, said,

'Strange is my name and I'm on strange ground. And strange it is that I can't be found.' They renamed the crick Strange Crick. And they renamed the town Strange, West Virginny." He looks down into his plate and steers another mouthful of stew into his hairy maw with a large soup spoon. "Never you mind, we know Willum Strange is still out there."

"So, you don't think those were his bones?"

"Mebbe they were. Mebbe they wernt." He looks back up at me wide eyed. "But *somebody's* still doing his work."

This is better than It's a Small World or The Haunted Mansion. I half expect to see translucent specters of lost souls down through the ages in period costumes seated along the wall around the room. "OK, I'll bite. What's his work?"

"He's watching over us. All of us. You, me. Barkeep." He looks over at the other patron. "Him." With his wide eyes fixed on me, he shovels another spoonful of stew into his mouth, spilling onto his beard, and then sucking along his lower lip trying to recapture as much spillage as possible. He places his spoon down on the table and leans closer. "There was one year, no rain, no crops. People on the verge of starvation. Winter coming. Willum Strange took a hunting party, four of the hardiest men in his holler and the next two or three hollers, they fixed to head down Elk River as far as need be to bring back enough game to last the winter—five men and three pack mules." He attempts once more to suck stew out of his beard along his lower lip. "They say they ran into Shawnee. But it could have just as easy have been Brits or French. They were all ready to kill settlers at the time. Whatever devilry they encountered, he lost all his men and one of the mules. Mebbe they et the mule, I don't know.

Whether they just scattered in the woods or got scalped, we'll never know for sure. But Willum Strange was a man of solid mountain principles. He was gonna take care of his people. He was gonna bring home food for his family and the families that sent their men with him. He was gonna avenge whatever foul dealin' they ran into down that river. And he wasn't gonna enjoy the comforts of his own bed until he brought home the men he led out thar." He extends his lower lip to suck his whiskers along his upper lip. "Willum Strange didn't return that winter. But somehow his family et fresh game all winter—until plantin' season. They say he would leave deer and rabbit on his family's doorstep. Wolves and bear would smell it and come roun', but they wouldn't touch it. His woman and his youngins would hear steps and sounds of heavy weights being drug up and down the trails outside their cabin, and they'd know he'd been there. Same with the other four families." He pulls back from me slightly.

He looks at my Pepsi can. "You know, that'll prolly cost you more than a whole jar of moonshine."

I look at the can, with distaste for the idea that I could have had a mason jar full of hundred-and-eighty-proof bathroom gin instead. "That's fine." I smile to myself. "I thought maybe if I drank the moonshine, I'd never be able to leave here, or something." I smile but he doesn't recognize my humor.

My companion lifts his head slightly with his eyes open even wider. "I hain't thought of that." His eyes returned to normal. "You can lose a day or two, I know that for a fact."

"Next you're going to tell me Willum Strange appears as a mountain man in buckskin with a Kentucky long rifle leading two mules along the river."

"You, sir, are a revelation!" My companion leans forward again. "You talk like you seen 'im! You seen 'im? You seen 'im?"

"I saw him on my way here. I-I mean I saw someone leading two mules along the river." I try to clear my head, feeling entranced. "You mean he's some kind of Robin Hood stealing from the rich and giving to the poor?"

"Nah." He shakes his head. "There's not rich enough to steal from round cheer. But mountain men are independent, self-sufficient. Honorable. God-fearin'." He leans down almost dipping his whiskers into his plate. "People still tell of his visits. One time, two peckerwoods from the city came through in a van. They saw a girl walking home from her shift at the Waffle Shop. They grabbed her. They had evil designs on her. They pulled off the road where they didn't think anyone could hear or see. Well, she screamed bloody murder, but when all was done, those two boys were gelded and half-skinned alive. That girl wandered back to the road and some passerby took her to the sheriff. She was ruffled and her clothes mussed, but her virtue was intact. He couldn't make heads nor tails of her story except, 'a knife as big as my arm!' The next day, the sheriff came across their van, and it all made sense. It was Willum Strange."

"So, you better make sure you don't run afoul of Willum Strange? Eh?"

"The god-fearing don't have to worry."

"You looked worried when I said I saw that man along the river."

"I just always shake at the prospect of encountering something from the next world." He looks dead-serious.

"Have a lot of people encountered Willum Strange?" I peer at him as the light from the wood stove plays on the side of his face I shades of red, yellow, and amber. "Any current-day, people you know, credible witnesses? Anyone who hasn't been drinking moonshine at the time?"

"Ask the barkeep. He's served him a dozen time." He tilts his head toward the bar.

From the bar, the barkeep's voice calls out, "You don't believe in Willum Strange?" He walks over to our table and continues in a low voice. "He walks in that door," he says, pointing toward the front of the room. "It gets airish, downright cold. He's tall, bushy red beard, thick red eyebrows." He pauses, his eyes going back and forth between the two of us at the table. Then, lowering his voice further, he continues intently, "Eyes like burning coals and breath like death. He leans his rifle against the bar and then he drives his hunting knife into the bar. Thwack!" He shifts on his feet. "Look for yourself, there must be fifty marks in that bar where he planted his knife. And then he says, 'Cat's head and gravy,' he pauses, and then, 'and a shine.'"

"Cat's head?"

"A flar biscuit the size of a cat's head." He looks back and forth between us. "I try to give him a little extra, if we got it. It's the thing to do when someone's watching over you." The barkeep looks back and forth between us at the table. His roving glance makes a third stop, and then he heads back to his place behind the bar. I follow his last glance and I'm startled to see that the other patron has come over and is listening intently to our conversation. Locking eyes with him for a long moment, he continues to stare, saying nothing. I turn my attention back to my companion across the table. I sit in silence. My dinner companion continues to clean his plate and his face. I contemplate this chord of superstitious belief, resistance to demystification or progress. I look forward to getting to Charleston and returning to the modern world.

Before I complete my thought, it seems, I glimpse out the front window and see parts of two grey mules. The door opens silently, revealing a tall thin figure backlit by the rising moon. The temperature in the room drops noticeably. The figure moves through the doorway. The bulletin board of tax and laundry services and the display table of t-shirts and shot glasses seems to recede, and he approaches the bar. He carefully leans an antique long rifle against the bar and then deftly withdraws a large Bowie knife from its sheath. And then tossing it lightly in the air, he catches it, changing his hand position, and then drives it into the wooden bar.

The barkeep, eyes turned down, attends him almost reverently. In a voice like a January blizzard, the figure says, "Cat's head and gravy." There was a moment of silence. And then, "'shine." The barkeep pours him a mason jar of moonshine from the jug under the bar and then retreats to the stove to prepare the order. For a timeless moment, the figure stands—almost seeming to float—in front of the bar. The room is silent except for the sound of the barkeep scooping ingredients and scraping the skillet.

I stare in my unbelief until finally the figure turns his head and looks directly at me, with eyes like two red-hot embers. His eyebrows and beard seem to writhe or radiate as though alive, while the weary head and body behind them seem weighed down, wracked with the pain of the ages. Instantly, I avert my eyes. Fear and reverence rumble over me like the preamble of a mountain thunderstorm. As my mind clears I see the sweet, proud faces of Rico and Esma Esteban. I feel the conviction that when I reach Charleston tonight, I will do so in the company of the host of good mountain people.

What Change the Cold Moon Brings

Neil felt the blood pounding in his ears as he entered his building, the Perdita Arms on Fourteenth Street. He felt that he'd been detected as soon as he crossed the threshold, and that Mrs. Serbouros, the building superintendent, the all-sensing guardian of the gates, the coffee-breathing, venom-jawed, hell hound was already scuttling in his direction, ready to indict, convict, and sentence him for his fated failings in one fell swoop. But he saw no one in the lobby and as the heavy inner vestibule door sealed tight behind him, he heard silence—not a footstep, not a breath. He walked gingerly past the door of the superintendent's apartment toward the elevator at the far end of the lobby. He could see the oxidized brass dial on the art deco floor indicator above the elevator door vibrating, pinned to the far right indicating "B" for basement. Before he could press the Up call button, he heard the distant rumble of machinery somewhere above his head, as if it were Hercules himself groaning under the burden of hauling this singular elevator car up from some nether realm. For some reason, basement-to-ground-floor was always the most burdensome transit for the old machinery. From the other side of the doors, he could hear the squeak and clank of the straining cables and the grind of the car returning to the ground floor.

Then with a foul odor of rancid beans, the doors parted to reveal Mrs. Serbouros, barely four feet tall and nearly four feet wide, dressed in what looked like a trench poncho from The Great War with her head wrapped in a vintage snakeskin print silk scarf.

"Good evening, Mr. Strohman." Mrs. Serbouros craned her neck to address Neil. "Mr. Strohman, I'm glad I caught you."

Without thinking, Neil waved his hand in front of his face to dispel the aroma of stale coffee. He stepped to the side and waited for Mrs. Serbouros to exit the elevator car, thinking, *Don't look into her eyes. Don't look into her eyes. She'll read your thoughts. She'll steal your soul. Whatever you do, don't look into her eyes*. He chafed with the courtesy.

"Mr. Strohman, you know you can't just leave a little one alone like that," she said as she stepped out of the elevator, eyes locked on Neil Strohman. "He's been fussing for half the day—since seven at least. I almost entered your apartment at one point, but just as I reached your door he quieted right down."

"I'm sorry, Mrs. Serbouros. I'll try to keep him quiet." Neil continued to avert his eyes, now trying to slip past Mrs. Serbouros and her unblinking stare. Sliding through the doors, Neil sought out the "3" button, and then hit "Close Door," "Close Door," "Close Door." Turning to face the doors, yet still looking at the floor to avoid her stare, he exhaled like a soldier fresh from the gauntlet. As the doors closed, he wondered at the strange way Mrs. Serbouros had spoken of Nacho, the puppy that Kaleigh had surprised him with a few days earlier. Nacho now waited for him in his apartment. Neil smiled thinking of the collie/shepherd mix with the heterochrome eyes—one brown, one blue. But if Mrs. Serbouros had now detected the dog, wouldn't she have gone right to citing the no-pet clause in his lease—or at least trying to hit him with an up-fee?

The elevator stopped, dinged, and opened its doors onto the third floor. Stepping out, Neil heard the distinct sound of a baby crying. Passing two apartments, his confusion mixed with anxiety as he heard a very un-canine human-sounding cry growing louder as he neared his own door. Fumbling with his keys, he burst into the apartment and in the same motion threw the door shut behind him. In four brisk steps he crossed the living room of his one-bedroom apartment and peered into the dog crate that now contained a baby lying on its back, wearing nothing but a very loose leather dog collar, waving arms and legs in supplication, voicing abject need, showing in its one brown eye and one blue eye glints of recognition at the sight of Neil.

"Nacho?!"

The urgency of the situation prevented Neil from processing the confusion, anxiety, and creeping wonder that flooded his brain. He wrestled the baby out of the crate, grasping him under the arms and glancing back down at the soiled cage liner. Locking eyes with the baby, he froze in thought, peering into the brown eye, the blue eye, and examining the nose, the chin, the brown leather collar, the chubby pink shoulders and arms, and the round torso dangling at arm's length. Shaking his head, he muttered, "No clue." He examined the belly button in the center of the round belly and then the hips and the inscrutable genitalia just as a stream of nearly clear liquid sprayed him directly in the chest. The sudden stream stirred him from his trance and he reverted to his native state of panic.

Bringing the naked babe over to his kitchenette, Neil laid him down on the cutting board. Thinking twice, he moved the child to the drainboard. He reached for his kitchen sponge and, lifting the child by one leg, he attempted to clean the soiled rear and thighs. Looking at the sponge, he threw it into the garbage. Holding the child down with one hand, he grabbed the only cloth he could reach—the dish-towels hanging on the oven door handle. Again, performing the one-leg lift, he positioned the towel under the child's rear and brought the towel up as a makeshift diaper between his legs and over the piss dispenser. Then, again holding the baby down on the drainboard with one hand, he reached down to open the junk drawer with the other. He pulled out a roll of duct tape and closed the drawer with his hip.

The child was now quiet, gazing at Neil with an adoring bemused wonder. Neil held him down gently with his fore-arm in order to apply both hands to the roll of tape. He tore off two pieces, one by one, tacking each to the edge of the counter. He then fastened the edges of the towel around the pudgy belly. Once the urgency of the moment passed, he removed the collar. Holding the eclectically dressed baby up over his drainboard, he breathed deeply and began to process what had just come into his life.

Hugging the baby to his chest, Neil walked over to his sofa and lay down, the baby's head resting on his shoulder. Part of him hoped and part of him wondered whether he might wake from this very strange dream.

◎

Neil woke very early Saturday morning with a moist sensation running along his collar bone and pooling at his throat. He felt the small weight of Nacho breathing in and out on his chest. Slowly Neil became aware of another sensation, mid-abdomen, of spreading warmth. Realizing sleep had not released him from this dream, he pinned the baby to his chest, securing the child's neck with his right hand, and the two rose as one from the sofa. Relying on the early morning light, he walked over to the kitchenette and surveyed the situation under the nightlight of the stove hood. He only had two more dishtowels—if they weren't already in the laundry. He was out of scrubbing sponges. He had a half roll of paper towels. The baby moved his head but didn't wake. He smacked his lips. Sensing a closing window of opportunity, Neil lowered the child onto the drainboard once again, pulled open the second drawer, relieved to see that he had one more clean towel, and repeated the previous night's diaper operation. Nacho still did not wake.

With one threat to world peace averted, one other loomed larger. What could he feed this—child? *How* could he feed him? Opening the refrigerator, he took inventory of four bottles of beer, two bottles of Gatorade, some sliced cheese, bologna, a jar of pickles, and in the door an opened pint of half-and-half left over from some recipe Kaleigh had made for him. The bag of puppy kibble atop the refrigerator stared down at him. Walking around to the bathroom, he switched on the light and opened the medicine cabinet. The baby squirmed under the fluorescence and opened his eyes, looking up at Neil. Neil locked eyes with the baby momentarily and instinctively began rocking him back and forth.

He peered into the cabinet. Knocking bottles and tweezers into the sink, Neil pulled out the rubber bulb he used for irrigating his ear wax. With one hand, without clearing the sink, he ran some water. Holding the bulb under the flow and squeezing it a couple times, he nodded his approval. Looking back down at the baby, he cooed, "That'll do. That'll have to do, won't it, Nacho?" Pouring the half-and-half into an NYU rocks glass, he tucked the bulb into his shirt pocket and carried the baby over to the ratty easy chair. He placed the glass on the side table, pulled the bulb out of his pocket, and then repositioned the baby in the crook of his left arm, moving his right arm through the motions of filling the bulb and bringing it over to the child's mouth and returning it. He then tried it for real, squeezing, dipping into the glass, releasing, and bringing it over to the baby's mouth. At first Neil tried forcing the liquid out of the bulb, but the infant gagged and brought it back up, sputtering. Eventually, Neil managed to hold it tip-down allowing the child to draw it out of the bulb. Soon Nacho closed his eyes and drifted off to sleep. Neil carefully crossed back to the sofa and lay back down without disturbing the baby. Using his left hand to secure the child, he reached over to the coffee table and retrieved his cell phone. He then stabilized the sleeping infant between his two arms and began to text:

TO> Kaleigh Sweet Cheeks

> You won't believe this.

Later that day, Neil recognized a bird-like knock at his apartment door: *ta ti-ti-ti*. Neil rose from his chair. Nacho continued to sleep peacefully on the sofa between two throw pillows. Neil peered through the peep hole before opening the door. Kaleigh carried two bags of groceries—diapers, wipes, bottled water, and a can of baby formula. "This better not be some kind of joke," she said in a quiet voice, "Because I spent real money on this stuff." She handed the groceries to Neil and hung her scarf and coat by the door. "Where's this quote unquote baby? Where's little Nacho?!"

Neil nodded toward the sofa and turned to place the groceries on the kitchen counter.

Kaleigh looked quizzically down at the baby on the sofa. She looked over at the empty dog crate. Her face filled with wonder. The child stirred, stretched its arms and legs, yawned, and opened its eyes—one deep brown, one bright blue. Kaleigh froze. In a gentle voice that testified to miracle manifest, she cooed, "Nacho!"

Kaleigh and Neal sat on the sofa flanking the sleeping infant, now dressed in a proper disposable diaper. Kaleigh leaned forward to grab a take-out box of pho noodles from the coffee table. Neil reached for a beer bottle. Kaleigh tapped a spork against her lower lip. "Maybe he's a changeling." Neil returned a puzzled look. "You know, a fairy being that changes shape to get into people's homes. Poses as a human child. Maybe this one posed as a dog. And he plans to cast a spell over us and take us away to his fairy realm."

"I think he's definitely cast a spell over *you*. But I didn't think you believed in stuff like that?"

Kaleigh looked down at the baby sleeping between them. "I don't think I have the option *not* to believe in things like that at this point." She looked into the face of the infant and cooed, "I have to believe in *you*, don't I, Nacho?"

"But what are the other options?" Neil interrupted the reverie. "Maybe he's a werewolf. Maybe he'll turn back into a mad dog on the next full moon and tear our throats out."

Kaleigh shook her head dismissively. "Didn't you notice? Last night *was* a full moon." She pointed out the window. "Look, it's right there, right there, the Cold Moon."

"The what?"

"The full moon that falls in December is called the Cold Moon. It's also called the Moon Before Yule or Long Night's Moon."

"Well, last night was certainly a long one for me."

"So, he turned from a dog into a baby when the full moon arrived, when the moon reached full illumination, I suppose. So maybe he's a . . . a were-*boy*? Is that a thing?" Kaleigh looked down at her phone, scrolling. The sleeping child shifted and turned his head, smacking his lips. "You said he was in baby form last night by dinnertime?"

"Mrs. Serbouros said she heard sounds of a baby fussing around seven."

"That's at least nineteen hours before the absolute full moon. So, if we're right, then he'll turn back around 11:30 tomorrow morning."

They looked at each other, not sure whether to feel better or worse. "Then we would have a pattern. We'd know how to live our lives."

"Yeah," Neil smiled slyly.

"What? What?!"

"I guess that makes you 'Nacho mama'."

Kaleigh shook her head. "I'm not *yo'* mama!" she said, turning to Neil.

"I would laugh at that if I weren't so confused." Looking back down at Nacho, he paused and then continued, "But that would make you his mama at least a couple days each month. Were-boy Mama."

"I don't know that mama's a part-time job . . ." She touched Nacho's hand. His fingers closed around her index finger. Neil felt as though unseen fingers were closing around his own throat.

The second night of the Cold Moon passed with two more feedings and two more diaper changes. Neil and Kaleigh took turns sleeping two or three hours at a time, standing watch on little Nacho.

Sunday morning arrived. Neil and Kaleigh slept the sleep of the jealous—jealous for every moment of oblivious slumber. As the appointed time approached, Kaleigh held the baby in her arms. Eleven. Eleven-thirty. Eleven-forty-five. Neil looked at the infant in Kaleigh's arms and wrinkled his brow. "Maybe we don't have it figured out? Maybe this is it. Maybe he's a boy from now on." Neil sounded disappointed.

The child opened his eyes, one brown, one blue. Alarm showed on his pink face. He stared up at Kaleigh and then searched for Neil. Neil edged toward Kaleigh. Together they looked down at Nacho.

"He's such an adorable peanut," Kaleigh whispered. "What's wrong little one?"

Neil looked from Kaleigh to Nacho. He felt the weight of the last two days and surrendered to the moment. He put his arm around were-mama and were-baby.

The child gave a cry and then began a muffled whimper. He stretched his arms and legs. Wisps of hair on his head began to noticeably thicken. Hair began to appear from around his shoulders, wrapping around his sides and finally covering his belly. His jaw and nose began to extend, and his limbs began to elongate. His fingers retracted into rough-textured pads. After several minutes, Nacho had returned to puppy form. He closed his jaws full of tiny needle teeth with play viciousness on Kaleigh's fingers. Neil replaced Nacho's collar and removed the diaper that they had placed on him just hours before. Sitting back down on the sofa, they looked at each other without a word as Nacho jumped back and forth between them, climbing on their legs and into their laps, testing his jaw strength on hands, clothes, ears, whatever he could close his mouth on. Neil wondered whether he didn't prefer the baby form. He could tell that Kaleigh did. "Let's walk him and get some fresh air."

Over the next twenty-six and a half days, Neil and Kaleigh talked increasingly about the weekend of the Cold Moon. Did it really happen? Had they been under some influence? It all seemed less real as time passed. And Nacho, with his sweet heterochrome face, could he really be some kind of . . . adorable monster that might some night kill them in their sleep? Every third or fourth day, their conversation would turn to the attempt to forecast if and then when. Because if it did, how do they keep it from Mrs. Serbouros. And Mrs. Serbouros seemed to be paying Neil more and more attention, with piercing glares whenever her eye caught him coming or going. She knew there was a baby in 3D. Did she also know there was a puppy? And to breach the fact that there was some kind of changeling was out of the question. He had a feeling that perhaps she knew more than he did. It was a month of anticipation and confusion.

The Wolf Moon approached—January 25th around 1:00 AM. Neil and Kaleigh were intent on learning as much as possible this time around. Neil and Kaleigh both took that Wednesday off from work to be with Nacho. Kaleigh estimated that the full moon approached full illumination about nineteen hours before the absolute full moon and passed by full illumination another nineteen hours after the astronomical full point. As the time approached, they sat at either end of Neil's sofa with puppy Nacho roaming back and forth between them. The sky was obscured by clouds. The moon was pale and low on the horizon. At 9:13 that morning, Nacho put his head down on his paws. He began panting, his heterochrome eyes took on a distant focus, and he began his transformation. In less than two minutes, he achieved the form of a plump pink baby.

During that process, Neil thought he heard a rough sniffing or snorting coming from under the door, as if someone or something were out in the hall, sensing them. But in front of him was a toddler. Under the full Cold Moon, Nacho had appeared to be a newborn or an infant no more than a few months old. He now appeared to be to have the body of at least a one-year-old.

Neil removed the collar. Kaleigh picked up the naked baby and carried him over to the kitchenette where the drainboard was now covered by a foam pad with diaper accessories conveniently adjacent. The child put up with the changing routine. Nacho began making sucking motions with his lips. The next question would be, *How much does a were-boy grow each month. How can they anticipate the needs of this monthly visitor?*

After being diapered, Nacho sat up suddenly all on his own. Neil and Kaleigh exchanged glances. Kaleigh hoisted him from the changing table and put him down on the living room floor. He crawled over to the sofa and steadied himself as he stood up. He began waving his arms and then landed again on his diapered bottom. In a matter of hours, he was crawling and standing, pointing and grasping, holding and shaking whatever he could get his hands on.

Neil asked, "Do you want to feed him?" Kaleigh nodded with a smile, seating herself in the chair. Neil handed Nacho to his were-mama. The baby looked around for the food source. He pushed away the bottle, continuing to look hungrily. "Plan B," Kaleigh announced. "Look in the cabinet next to the microwave." Neil found jars of baby food along with a small spoon. "Bring me one of those jars," she called, "And the spoon." Kaleigh settled into the chair and shifted the baby's position to sitting upright on her lap. Taking the jar and spoon from Neil, she began the feeding. Neil seemed to see a certain glow about her as she fed little Nacho. Once feeding was done, she put the empty jar down on the table along with the spoon and took up the book on top of the pile—*One Fish Two Fish Red Fish Blue Fish*. She began to read in a low tone.

Hop On Pop followed *One Fish Two Fish Red Fish Blue Fish*, followed by a chapter of *Eat Pray Love.* Nacho began to nod off. Before long, Nacho was asleep. Neil moved him carefully to the sofa bolstered by throw pillows. Neil met

Kaleigh in the middle of the room. Taking her face in his hands, he kissed her gently. "Caring for a baby can be very sexy." Wrapping his arms around her, he started to pull the back of her shirt out of her jeans. As if on cue, Nacho sat up straight and his face turned red. He began to pant.

"You know what the means?" asked Kaleigh.

"He's not due to turn back to a puppy, so that must be diaper time."

"Babies can be very frustrating," she says, brushing Neil's hair out of his face.

Nacho, red-faced, gave a long low grunt.

"Is this our lives now? Are you comfortable with this be-ing our lives?" Kaleigh searched Neil's face. "You know this was never on my list. But I'm not walking away."

Neil nodded and said in a low voice, "You never planned on having a cryptid baby?" He glanced down. "But I'm not walking away either. We'll do this together?"

"We'll do this together." She smiled, "And don't ever call our little angel a cryptid!"

Between the two of them, they managed one more diaper change, and then Kaleigh put on her coat and collected her things. "You're taking tomorrow off, but I still have to work." Standing by the door, she looked down at Neil who was lying on the floor next to Nacho. "You think you'll be ok with him tomorrow?" Neil nodded. "OK, I'll see you around dinner time. Maybe we can walk him." She punctuated the sentence with a nod of her head. She disappeared through the door.

Neil turned his head back to his charge who was rolling over, pushing himself up onto all fours, looking for whatever he might grab or climb. Neil felt his world becoming very close.

◙

February's Snow Moon showed more drastic advances. Nacho appeared to be the size of a two- or even three-year-old. He would grab at his diapers and clothing as someone tried to dress him, though he still needed help to get dressed properly. He was now standing, walking, waving, talking in streaks.

But more striking than his physical development was his mental advancement. It appeared clear to Neil that puppy Nacho had been listening to everything, registering what he heard even though he couldn't speak it in puppy form. Almost as soon as he baby-formed with the Snow Moon, he began trying to say words he had heard as a puppy. Almost immediately, he had said his first words, addressing Kaleigh as "Mama" and addressing Neil as "Nana." Of course, Kaleigh began calling Neil "Nana" as well.

Within a day he had started to repeat phrases from nursery rhymes or books that Kaleigh or Neil read to him. He was saying colors, but confusing red, green, brown, pink, and purple. He was counting to four. He was tapping on the window wanting to go outside. At the park he recognized dogs that he had met on his own walks as a dog, but he looked at them with a strange curiosity. He kept crouching down to sniff their butts. He was ready to run and use his arms in ways he'd seen other children using them—ways that he couldn't do in his puppy form—like picking things up and throwing them.

After a frenetic two days and a transformation back to puppy form, a tired Nacho sat next to a tired Neil, leaning against him, looking up at him with unconditional love and devotion. Neil looked down at Nacho and thought to himself, *You're looking at me like that, like I'm the center of your world. If you lived your whole life as a dog, you might always look at me like that. In a few more moons, you might start to think more like a human, and you might carry that thinking with you when you return to your dog body. I wonder whether you'll look at me with that same love and devotion at that point. Will you be able to see me as your human or will you be conscious that I'm flawed and imperfect—one more self-interested person playing the same old games?*

The moons and months passed faster and faster: the Worm Moon on March 25th, the Pink Moon on April 23rd, the Flower Moon on May 23rd.

With each month, Nacho reached new milestones. He was running. He was into everything, searching for food, toilet paper, anything he could throw. He was talking a blue streak, talking so fast no one could understand him. Neil and Kaleigh had to repeatedly ask him, "Slow down, talk slower." He was fascinated with the TV remote. And books. He wanted to know how they worked. And he was fascinated by music. He would dance wildly. His speech was eerily clear and distinct. Neil realized that what he was hearing while in dog form was being retained. He was a sponge. And his heterochrome gaze showed great and constant intensity.

Kaleigh and Neil, usually together, would take him to Jackson Park. He would approach children at the playground. There was still some awkwardness around other children and other dogs. He didn't have words for it yet, but he was forming the question 'Why am I different?'

As May's Flower Moon approached, Nacho continued to expand his vocabulary; he went into the refrigerator to try to feed himself; he went into the pantry cabinet to get dog treats.

Mrs. Serbouros commented more than once that she never saw the dog and the child together. *What do you know, woman?* Neil thought to himself. *What do you know?* And then one day, as they were passing Mrs. Serbouros in the lobby, Nacho blurted out, "You know, I'm a were-boy!"

Neil mumbled, "Kids' imaginations. You know."

Mrs. Serbouros smiled, "I know, I know." She looked up at Neil without a smile. "He's walking and talking—at the age of five months? I know." She seemed to smile genuinely. "Every once in a while our kind does come along."

"You're uh-h-h," Neil stammered.

"Not exactly." She shook her head, "Not exactly. Some of us age at different rates." She looked Neil in the eye, "And sadly some of us aren't touched by time at all. We can only wish that time would take us. We're destined to stand our posts. But sometimes we still marvel at what we witness."

Nacho waved to Mrs. Serbouros as they moved out the door. She waved back smiling, watching him go.

With the arrival of the Strawberry Moon, on June 21st, Nacho transformed just after 9:00 that evening. Nacho seemed to have had an intellectual growth spurt, no doubt responding to Neil and Kaleigh reading to him and Kaleigh bringing him audio books. Having bought *Bridges of Madison County* for herself, Kaleigh sat down and played it out loud for Nacho. He acted like he'd been hit by lightning. He would sprawl on his back with his legs in the air listening to *David Copperfield, Great Expectations*, and *Heart of Darkness*. And with the Sturgeon Moon, on August 19th, it was time to sit him down and talk with him about school: He would have to be home-schooled. He couldn't go to a regular school; people wouldn't understand.

"But you two understand. And Mrs. Serbouros understands. Why won't other people understand?"

"Nacho." Kaleigh searched for words. "Some people have trouble understanding people who aren't like them."

"And some people," Neil added, "Are just afraid of things they don't understand."

"Why aren't there others like me?" Nacho pleaded. "Why?! You can't tell me that in all of New York City there aren't other were-boys or were-girls. Why aren't there others like me?!"

Nacho was upset and angry for the rest of the weekend. Nevertheless, Neil pressed ahead with his education. Neil tried to talk with him about the birds and the bees.

"No duh! Of course, I know all that." Nacho wouldn't look at Neil. He sat with his arms folded. "You know I can smell things when I'm a dog. I can tell who's gotten it and how recently. I can tell who's in heat and who's looking for some. I'm not a simpleton."

"Then you know you have to practice self-control. People —"

"People won't understand?! I don't *care* if anyone else under*stands!*" Nacho jumped to his feet and ran into the bathroom, slamming the door. The topic was never revisited. But the remainder of the weekend, Nacho acted out his displeasure, eating crayons, urinating on the carpet in front of Neil and Kaleigh, and finding other ways to express his hostility. Nacho started these behaviors as a boy and continued over the next several weeks as a dog.

As a distraction, or perhaps a peace offering, Kaleigh bought him a new collection of audio books—Shakespeare.

By the time of the Corn Moon, the evening of September 17th, there were clear signs of hormones and puberty. And the Hunter Moon and Beaver Moon of October and November saw dramatic increases in his vocabulary and the depth of his thought and expression.

In a quiet moment, Neil asked, "How different is it? You know, when you're in dog form versus when you're in your human form?"

"There are some major differences," Nacho said, gazing out the window, collecting his thoughts. "It's the same but different. Some things are less prominent." He paused, struggling to put it into words. "In my human body, sight, the world in full color, vision is foremost. In my dog body, reds become greys. Pinks and purples become greys. Greens become browns. I can still see blues and yellows. It's like I see blues and yellows the same and everything else becomes background shapes in shades of grey. But the big difference is that while my view of the world is diminished, there's another . . . dimension of . . . of information layered on top of it. Scent and taste actually create a map of the world more vivid than sight. It's almost visible, the way my sense of smell is amplified. It's like I can smell something and almost see what any particular scent came from. I can know what that thing smelled like yesterday and a week ago and what it will probably smell like tomorrow. I can pick up scents farther away than I can see. It's like, I can smell the entire world at once, but I can only see a little piece of it. I can smell sickness and know what area of a body that sickness is connected to. I can tell by scent what foods are good for that particular sickness and what foods are bad for that sickness. My hearing gets more powerful, too. But not as much as my sense of smell. I can smell blood. Smell sweat. Smell stress and fear. I can smell sexual activity. I can tell who got some with whom and when."

"I remember you saying that."

"Yeah, I know what goes on around here. Around this whole building." A cloud crossed his face.

Nacho sat quietly for a moment and then continued, "There's another difference, too. When I'm in my dog body, the world is one—no distinctions. Except that you are the most important thing—you and Kaleigh. But now, when I'm in my boy body, it's like there's me, and then there's you and other people, and then there's God—sometimes I feel the divine presence. As a dog, I just smell and hear and see Creation."

The Hunter's Moon arrived the morning of October 17th. Nacho's first question upon taking boy form was "What's this Santas Claus crap?" Nothing was said about it either way. Kaleigh invited Nacho to go grocery shopping. He declined. When Kaleigh got home, she found Nacho passed out on the floor. "He raided the fridge," she updated Neil later. "It looks like he had three beers and then threw up next to the sofa and fell asleep on the floor."

"You're not the boss of me!" Nacho called from the dark bedroom.

"I'm just glad he didn't wake up and start licking up his own vomit," Kaleigh shared with Neil.

"How do you know he didn't?"

◎

The Beaver Moon arrived just before dinnertime on November 15th. Immediately, Nacho said, "I'm going to take a walk."

Neil put down his book to go with him.

"Oh, of course, you're coming with me, aren't you?" Nacho said with venom.

They walked around the block to Jackson Park. Nacho seemed inattentive to their usual conversation. Suddenly he held up his hand to Neil. "Stay here a minute." He was focused on two girls, perhaps college age, walking and chatting. He walked intentionally across the grass. As he approached the two girls he circled around them. They turned to watch this strange behavior. He bowed playfully. The girls seemed to be amused. They exchanged words at more than an arm's length. The girls continued to smile and laugh. Nacho gradually got closer. Suddenly he reached out and tugged on the lapel of the coat of one of the girls. The girls stepped back, seeming alarmed. They then said something loudly, angrily, and walked off at a brisk pace, looking back with arms around each other. Nacho watched them go. Neil walked over to the spot where Nacho stood.

"Didn't go well?" Neil asked.

Nacho couldn't look at Neil. They resumed their walk, not looking at each other. After an interval, Nacho said, "'A dreamer is one who can only find his way by moonlight.'"

"Shakespeare?"

"Oscar Wilde."

As the December Cold Moon loomed, Neil and Kaleigh took stock of the situation they had been dealing with for a full lunar year, living with this peculiar member of their family. Nacho in boy form seemed to have the intellectual maturity of a twelve-year-old boy, and in other ways he seemed more like a sixteen-year-old. His height was what you might expect of a teenager. His weight, less so, making him rather thin and lanky. His language skills were very good, but his pronunciation was a little affected and stilted, no doubt due to his intense consumption of audio books. His ability to understand mathematical concepts was insightful, even intuitive.

Perhaps most acutely, Nacho would run to his crate where he felt safe whenever he was stressed. If Neil was stepping out and couldn't take Nacho in human form, Nacho would go into his crate and pull the door behind him. When becoming a boy, he would at first want to tug on toys and fetch frisbees, running back to drop them at Neil's feet. Turning back into a dog after almost two days of boy-time, he would want to throw frisbees and balls, at first pawing at the toys and then grabbing them in his mouth and shaking his head to cast them a few feet. He would then hang his head.

Nacho seemed to suffer a certain lack of confidence, not having community other than his parents to reinforce his choices. Kaleigh and Neil tried, but it seemed Nacho was passing beyond the point where, in boy form at least, he could not just accept his parents' affirmations. He would occasionally start a low howl until he heard a muted answer from somewhere below.

As Nacho's third Cold Moon approached, it was clear that each year was passing faster and faster. Neil was 29. Nacho was approaching an equivalent level of maturity. Nacho was listening to Plato, Machiavelli, and Thomas Merton. It was obvious that Nacho had discovered argument.

Every dog morning, Neil walked with Nacho, sharing what was on his mind. Neil would take advantage of Nacho's ability to retain information gathered while in dog form. Other people walking their dogs might talk on the phone or chat with some walking companion. Neil would be speaking to his dog about banking and job skills and household responsibilities. Occasionally, Nacho would turn his head and give Neil an agreeable or disagreeable "Ruh" or "Ruh-uh" or even register his exception by stopping in his tracks in response to something Neil said. On human days, Nacho would unload all his responses to Neil's monologues, with Neil often unable to get a word in. Neil and Nacho developed these long serial talks, about life's deep questions.

It was in Nacho's third Flower Moon when Nacho pushed Neil on a topic he seemed to be missing. "Hey, Neil, why don't you make it official? Why don't you ask Kaleigh to marry you?" It carried the weight of something coming from an equal, a peer. "Until you do, she'll be like the moon: Part of her always hidden away."

"Shakespeare?"

"I was actually paraphrasing Dia Reeves in *Bleeding Violet,*" said Nacho, schooling Neil. "Ask yourself what you're holding back and why. And what are you forcing her to hold back. Make yourself whole. Invite her to become whole. Stop treating her like a hired hand." The two walked in silence for once feeling the weight of Nacho's questions. As they approached their building in silence, Nacho stopped and turned to Neil. "'Everyone is a moon and has a dark side which he never shows to anybody.'"

"Shakespeare?"

"That was Mark Twain."

"Then what's the Shakespeare line about 'O swear by the fickle moon'?"

"That's Juliet telling Romeo not to make promises that she can't rely on—that change like the moon. She wants to know that she can count on Romeo."

In Nacho's fourth year, his temperament was clearly mellowing and ripening. He surpassed Neil in book knowledge and the wisdom of the sages. Anyone listening to their conversations—Neil at thirty, Nacho with the appearance of forty—would have taken Nacho to be the older brother, the uncle.

Neil didn't notice the grey appearing in Nacho's temples and chin. As they walked side by side, he may not have noticed his face flinching from pain. But inside Nacho was recognizing the limitations of his nature. He realized that more and more of their topics of conversation were really issues for Neil—decisions that Nacho would never have the chance to make for himself.

On his fourth Beaver Moon, as they walked along the city streets, their conversation flagged. Nacho was focused on the sidewalk. "'We are such stuff as dreams are made on, and our little life is rounded with a sleep.'"

"Now *that* is Shakespeare!" Neil smiled to himself having correctly identified the line. "I know that's Shakespeare." They came to the corner and waited for the walk signal.

On the first night of Nacho's fifth Strawberry Moon, Neil and Nacho followed their usual path. Nacho was quiet. When they reached the park, they sat and admired the moon that had risen just hours before. Nacho spoke, "'The moon shines bright. In such a night as this. When the sweet wind did gently kiss the trees and they did make no noise, in such a night.'"

"Shakespeare?"

"Of course." Nacho spoke again after a moment. "When I first heard that line, it meant nothing to me. But somehow tonight it seems full of meaning." He looked at Neil. "I don't think I'll ever know a moment so perfect as this. I'm glad I'm here to experience it with you."

"Me, too."

Neil had noticed that Nacho had been mentioning minor physical issues. His eyesight was not as keen as it once was. He had aches and pains when he tried to do what he used to do. Neil had been in denial about the obvious fact that Nacho, his adopted son, would probably pass before him.

"Neil, I want you to realize something before you get to where I am, where you can see the end approaching." Nacho looked at Neil intently with his heterochrome stare. "We live on the dry periphery of a watery orb that circles a ball of fire while a shining rock moves the seas back and forth—and you don't believe in miracles. Your life, like everything else in this world, should keep going in its current course, only slowing down as time passes. Anything else is a miracle. Open your eyes."

"Well, you're . . ."

"Not just me. Sometimes it's as if my existence has blinded you to every other miracle in your life. I should have *opened* your eyes to every other miracle in your life."

Before the Strawberry Moon had passed, Neil and Kaleigh were engaged, and they had made plans to get married on Nacho's next Strawberry Moon.

In Nacho's sixth year, he grew noticeably greyer and slower. Neil was thirty-two. Nacho looked like he was more than twice Neil's age. Nacho was starting to shrink, becoming a little old man, a little old dog. His complaints became more frequent and more severe. His speech more halting. His breathing more labored. His eyesight more clouded. His recall now slower.

Nacho seemed very pleased by the wedding in June. It wasn't a big affair, but it did take a little planning. For two or three months, Neil and Kaleigh were focused on the wedding.

However, it seemed that only a few weeks afterward, Nacho was again regressing—becoming again dependent like a child. The parent-child relationship was again flipping. Neil would sit and Nacho would lean against him and look up with his greying hair and his pallid skin and his heterochrome gaze. Neil could see pain in Nacho's eyes and he could feel Nacho breathing, irregular and labored. They now spent more time sitting on the benches in the park than walking—or chasing squirrels. Neil still discussed issues and asked advice, but more as a courtesy now. Nacho's man state seemed to grow closer to his dog state. The look in Nacho's eyes told him that even in Nacho's failing state, he wanted nothing more than to sit there with Neil on that bench. Neil wondered how many more moons he would have to share times like this with Nacho. Time was now precious. "I'm glad you married Kaleigh." Nacho looked around at children, squirrels, mothers with strollers. "Do you ever wonder what would have happened if Kaleigh had never surprised you with me?"

"I know what would have happened. I would have continued worrying myself about things that didn't matter."

Nacho's sixth year drew to a close with a series of grim reminders of cold reality—arthritis, incontinence, mental lapses. Neil and Kaleigh talked about the fact that if Nacho were just a regular dog, they would be talking about putting him down. But clearly that was not an option. They would struggle through the ignominy of his old age regardless of what that brought.

Nacho's sixth Cold Moon came. Outside it was bitterly cold, but inside the Strohman apartment it was warm and homey. Kaleigh had news that she had not yet shared—good news.

Nacho's transformation on this moon brought with it marked pain and discomfort. Nacho was clearly suffering.

"Can I get you anything?" Kaleigh asked.

"Get Mrs. Serbouros."

"I'll call." Neil dialed the super's apartment and listened to it ring. The answering message came on, "This is building superintendent Serbouros. Leave a message. [Beep.]"

"Mrs. Serbouros, this is Neil Strohman in apartment 3D —."

There came a loud knock at the door. Kaleigh opened the door and looked down. "It's me!" It was Mrs. Serbouros. "I brought a wheelchair."

Neil hung up the phone.

Mrs. Serbouros scanned the room for Nacho. Spotting him by the window, she addressed him. "Nacho, is it time?"

"I think so." Nacho nodded. His face flinched with a wave of pain. "Yes, it's time."

Neil walked over to stand next to Nacho. "Where are you taking him?"

"Mister and Missus Strohman, you've done your part. Now I have to do mine. I'm the only one who can do this with him."

Neil looked down at Nacho with a questioning look.

Nacho closed his eyes and nodded.

Mrs. Serbouros wheeled the chair over to where Nacho sat. She lifted him and moved him over to the chair like he was a baby.

"But where are you taking him?" Neil repeated.

Peering over the wheelchair, Mrs. Serbouros said in a comforting voice, "Mister Strohman, it's not for you to know." She paused as if waiting for her statement to register. "It's my part to take care of him." After she was satisfied with the impact of her announcement, she wheeled him out of the apartment and down the hall to the elevator. Neil and Kaleigh stood at their door and watched as Mrs. Serbouros rolled Nacho into the elevator. Neil thought he saw a tail swishing from beneath her housecoat. She turned the chair around. The Strohmans saw Nacho for the last time as the doors closed. The machinery somewhere up above began to moan. The down arrow on the hall lantern flashed and the arm on the indicator dial swung from 3 to 2 to 1 and then finally all the way to B.

While We Were Still Enemies

Thursday was the third-best happy hour of the week and the clock had just struck four. Students and research assistants were streaming out of Room L-106 in the CUNY Advanced Research Center and down along Saint Nick Terrace toward West 130th Street as if fleeing a sinking ship. The lab grew quiet except for the gentle hum of refrigeration and the whir of electronics. Doctor Elmo Klein-Weiss, faculty director of the lab, sat at the central workstation holding Ophelia. He was ostensibly monitoring her vital signs and checking her stress levels. She was basically doing the same for him.

A familiar backpack appeared silently in the sidelight next to the door and the top of a wool beanie could be seen in the small square window in the door itself. The door buzzed and Juwan Jeffreys bustled into the lab. Ten minutes earlier he had been part of the exodus. Juwan's an undergrad at CUNY—earnest, sometimes irritating, but more often endearing. Doctor Klein-Weiss might say more often irritating than endearing.

Juwan waved sheepishly, "Hey, Doctor K-Dub!"

"Let me guess: they canceled happy hour for lack of interest? Harlem's run out of beer? You're on the wagon?"

"Yuh, no. Forgot my wallet," Juwan answered sheepishly. He skip-skated around tables and chairs to the workstation on the far side of the lab where one jacket hung on the back of one chair. Juwan patted the inside pocket. He smiled to himself and then with jacket in hand he bowed his head to the doctor, waving his wallet in silent apology.

"Happy hour is saved!" Doctor K-Dub feigned celebration while continuing to gaze down at Ophelia. "The earth continues to spin! We'll get to see another day!"

"Actually, happy hour'll probably be over before I get back to Rodrigo's." Juwan glanced down at his phone.

"Oops, I spoke too soon. News flash: life as we know it snuffed out at Rodrigo's."

Jacket in hand, Juwan paused awkwardly in front of the doctor. "But I wanted to talk to you anyway about the rebel gene."

The doctor froze and then tilted his head to look up at Juwan. "Okay, I give up. What are you talking about?"

"The adolescent development study on rats."

The doctor raised an eyebrow and then responded, "The adolescent development study focuses on brain activity and calls for collecting EEG data from rats; it's physiological, not genomic. What're you talking about—a rebel gene?"

Juwan cleared his throat and stood up straight, raising his hand to his chest in mock formality. "The rebel gene hypothesis, which I intend to make the focus of my Ph.D. thesis, is thus: A key element of personality development is triggered by the activation and expression of a gene I call the rebel gene which elicits identity opposition—not just differentiation, but direct opposition of the emerging offspring identity to the parental identity."

"So, you're looking for a correlation between the brain activity data that we're collecting in the current study and an associated specific gene activation that you intend to identify in a future study? You know how clear a correlation you'll need to prove an association like that? Any evidence supporting your hypothesis? Or any proposed experiment design that might collect it?"

"Yes!" Juwan was suddenly energized, his eyes wild and his smile electric. "Yes! From the adolescent development study that you and Milton began a week ago! I was planning to show it to you tomorrow—one data series in particular and one test subject so far—Horatio, I think."

"Okay," the doctor's voice waivered. "That's what science is all about, testing ideas. But it's late—in work-study hours. If you're scheduled in the lab tomorrow, let's look at it then, like you said." He nodded his head dismissively. "Have a good night, Juwan."

Juwan waved awkwardly and headed out the door into the hallway. His head disappeared from the square in the door and then his body and backpack passed by the sidelight. All sign of him gone but for the muffled rhythm of his trainers receding down the hall.

Looking back down at Ophelia, Doctor Klein-Weiss spoke soothingly, "You know Juwan is the reason you're here, right?" Ophelia wriggled her pink nose and gave several short demure squeaks.

Juwan had taken delivery of the last shipment of test subjects from Fishkill Rattery. Only faculty and authorized grad students had signing authority. Juwan was neither authorized nor trained to check the contents of a lab shipment of any kind. Fishkill Rattery had a purchase order for twenty-four class-A white Rattus norvegicus—standard-genome white Norway rats commonly referred to as fancy rats. Instead, they'd delivered twenty-three fancy rats and one albino. Anyone with experience with fancy rats would spot the error immediately. Properly bred fancy rats have black eyes and black noses against a white coat—sort of a white-tux / black-tie look. Albino rats have no pigment. Their eyes and noses only appear pink due to blood vessels close to the skin. Albinos also tend to have weak vision—deficiencies in the back of the eye resulting in a blurry, light-flooded world. Using albinos as test subjects can skew results—or worse, open your work up to peer criticism. But more importantly, returning anything to Fishkill Rattery causes the kind of headache that Doctor Elmo Klein-Weiss doesn't need to experience more than once in his lifetime. The Doctor vowed never again to pay restocking fees, post-origination fees, or penultimate destination fees to Fishkill Rattery if his life depended on it.

Ophelia would have to be excluded from the intended experiments, but Doctor Elmo Klein-Weiss would watch over her and manage her EEG cycles to make sure she could be used for some other one-off application in the lab. After all, a pedigreed, early-life-isolated A-class-genome Rattus norvegicus can cost in the triple digits. Waste not, want not.

Doctor Klein-Weiss looked down at Ophelia, gazing into her pink eyes. He'd been holding her gently but firmly in his two hands this whole time. Her irises enlarged as he gave her his full attention. Her limpid pink eyes were completely without guile or scheme—or maybe they were just unable to focus on the doctor's features. Ophelia had the pinkest of little pink noses. She twitched and wiggled her little pink rhinarium—the moist hairless part of the nose. She had a pleasing and shapely philtrum—that line—more of a trough in humans—that runs from the base of the nose down to the roof of the upper lip. In rodents it's known to control whisker motility, manipulating key sensing organs, and heightening odor sensations by adding moisture to in-coming airflow. Doctor Klein-Weiss recalled from six years of Hebrew school: every baby is taught all knowledge in the womb, but before a baby is born an angel taps them on the mouth making them forget all. The philtrum is said to be the mark left by the tap of the angel's finger. Ophelia must have been tapped by the daintiest of angels. Her nostrils and alar folds—the fleshy cowling that surrounds the nostril openings—possessed an alluring proportionality and symmetry. Her nasal tubercles were delicate but generous. Her nares—the side vents that some vertebrates use for exhaling —were exquisite. Rats aren't mouth-breathers. Mouth-breathing prevents collection of olfactory information while exhaling. In through the nostrils, out through the nares, resulting in a steady stream of information-rich smells.

Her eyes lined up perfectly with the bottoms of her ears, pink and gently rounded. As he cradled her in his two hands and drew her close, her whiskers formed an almost perfect radial circle extending from her nose to the tips of her ears and the ends of the ceramic electrode caps that sat on top of her head—white with red tips, like a fitting fascinator for a day at Saratoga Springs, Doctor Klein-Weiss thought, as if he would ever attend the races at Saratoga Springs.

Then the doctor reached across the desk and tapped the keyboard with his right hand, and in the twitch of a whisker, the cartoon rodent screensaver that scurried from one edge of the screen to another vanished. In the same smooth motion, the doctor picked up the scan gun and pointed it at Ophelia's fascinated head. He pulled the trigger and the gun scanned the electrodes implanted in her brain. All data since the last scan instantaneously uploaded and appeared on the right-hand monitor in color-coded waves, peaks and valleys, sensations and reactions, thoughts and urges, dreams and visions. Instantaneously, the graphic representation of everything that innocent Ophelia thought or experienced over the last night and day—her very essence—was laid bare on the screen before the Doctor.

"I think you just need some exercise. What? The other rats don't socialize with you? I know you're in separate cages, but you can't chat with them?" She gave a longer squeak. "Oh, you do?" he said, pretending to share a language. "Good. So, what's causing the heightened activity I see in data series seven?" Ophelia gave a short squeak. "You're coordinating hearing and vocalization. Are you talking to me, now?" He looked directly into her face. She gave another short squeak. "So now we're bonding?" Ophelia gave one more short squeak.

He looked back into her face. She made a soft huffing sound as she smacked her lips and began bruxing—grinding her front teeth in a slow, self-soothing rhythm—the rat version of purring. Doctor Klein-Weiss' brain was flooded with vasopressin, oxytocin, and a small amount of testosterone triggering parental instincts, attachment, and protectiveness—yes, they were bonding. Doctor Klein-Weiss smiled. Ophelia wiggled her waif-like philtrum, sensing in detail Doctor K-Dub's hormonal cocktail, and stared nebulously back at the blurry escarpment facing her.

Dr. Klein-Weiss exited the building shortly after five o'clock. Stepping into the scent and sound of the city, he glanced to his left. The shrubs along the front of the building had been freshly trimmed revealing white plastic boxes the size of cigarette cartons. The two-inch round holes at one end identified them as rat traps. These same traps in white or black models hide in plain sight behind every fast-food or coffee shop drive-through lane, neighborhood restaurant or apartment building parking lot. Inside the lab, rats are valuable test subjects. Outside, they are unwanted—threats to the health and the very operation of businesses. Where there are traps, there are nests—typically beneath half-dollar-sized tunnels running alongside utility conduits. Within a couple feet of the main entrance of each nest, there are usually one or more dash-holes—emergency exits often covered by dry leaves, shrubs, or other camouflage. And their scent marks and yellow grease streaks along walls leave clear evidence of the course of the actual rat race—clear enough to other rats and observant humans. "What a different world," Doctor Klein-Weiss thought to himself. "And what a different life, separated by a matter of feet. Inside the lab, rats can live up to three years, and just outside this door they're lucky to make it a full year. A regular tale of two cities."

Tonight, Elmo's commute home to Tarrytown took forty minutes. Miriam usually meets him at the door with her run-of-the-mill non-urgent complaints. Elmo, can you believe that plumber didn't even clean up after himself? I wait hours for him to show up, and he's in and out in twenty minutes—you wanna guess what *that* cost? I'm all done ma'am! And who's left to scrub his footprints off the bathroom floor? The lamb chops were subpar; do you think Matt Weinberg thinks because he winks at me he can give me subpar lamb chops? Subpar! And why do we even pay for cable subscriptions? We still have to pay extra for a movie or a show! What sense does that make, I ask? What sense?

But when Elmo came through the door, Miriam met him without a word. Immediately grasping the situation, Elmo said with false pleasantness, "Good evening, Miriam. How was *your* day?" He pushed on past the silent storm cloud staring up at him, put down his briefcase and hung up his raincoat, and then proceeded to peruse the stack of mail.

With hands on hips, Miriam once again maneuvered to place herself in front of him. "Elmo!" She looked around with a huff. "Elmo! Look at me. Look at me!"

Elmo looked up from the handful of envelopes and said nothing, sensing the pointlessness of any response on his part.

"Elmo! Be honest with me." And then the tears started.

Elmo steered her into the dining room and eased her into a chair. He then pulled a chair over for himself. He took a paper napkin from the art deco napkin caddy and held it out to Miriam, wondering what's gotten her so worked up this time. An inattentive shoe salesman? The line at the dry cleaners?

"Tell me, Elmo, is there some *bimbo* working in your lab or at the college—some *shiksa* who's making eyes at you—some office manager handling your private business—some work-study *homewrecker* offering to be of *service*?" She took the napkin and blew her nose.

Elmo contemplated her middle-aged but shapely philtrum and then took another napkin from the caddy.

Miriam continued, "I need you to be honest with me. I'm not going to have one of these sham marriages where she does her scrapbooking and he does his sudoku. I won't have it!"

Elmo was first touched by the genuine emotion in Miriam's complaint. And then he began to process the content of her question. "Bimbo? Shiksa?" He was about to answer the first or second part of her question and caught himself when he realized the direction of the third part. "No, Miriam. No, there is no homewrecker working to break up our happy nest."

Miriam looked into his eyes, dabbing her own eyes with the new napkin wrapped around her index finger. "I want to believe you, Elmo." She sniffed. "But I just can't take it if there's any truth to it. Any truth at all."

"To what? What's *it*?"

"What's *it*?! Maybe it's some hussy asking you questions and then acting thankful when you give them an *obvious* answer. Or touching your arm or your shoulder when they speak to you. Or complimenting you on your *lab coat* or your *sansabelt slacks*. I've seen this on *Maury*. What's *it*? What's *it*!"

"That's it?"

"Okay, then. It's you—taking longer and longer to get home each day. It's—it's you," and she began crying loudly, "it's you calling out her name in your sleep!" Miriam continued bawling.

"Miriam . . . Houston, we have a problem, come in Miriam."

She blurted out, "Last night you said 'Ophelia, Ophelia'—*twice*!" She could barely breathe, sup-supping. Elmo held and patted the hand that wasn't clenching the napkin. She gradually caught her breath and then said softly, "You said it so sweetly and tenderly, the way you used to say *my* name," and she took in a large breath in three parts and then continued at renewed volume, "when we were first mar-ri-i-i-i-i-ied!" She inhaled loudly and rhythmically as she tried to catch her breath.

Elmo said quietly, "She's a rat."

"Yes, she's a *rat*! She's a lousy *stinkin'* rat! She's—"

"Miriam, Miriam," he insisted quietly, "Ophelia's a lab rat." He smiled into her red eyes and runny pink nose.

Miriam wiped her upper lip and looked up at Elmo. "I had to call the plumber again today."

The Friday morning alarm and snooze came and went. Elmo sleepwalked in and out of the shower. He became aware of his surroundings as he lathered up to shave. He wiped the mirror with the side of the hand that held his razor. Leaning forward to present his face to the mirror, he readied himself in rote fashion for his first downward stroke from nose to lip. He stretched his upper lip over his teeth to get the cleanest result and suddenly he felt a tingling, a faint electrical impulse shooting from his philtrum to somewhere deep in his brain—somewhere between his ears. He followed that stroke by cleaning up his upper lip, stretching his lip one way and then the other. He felt another tingle. He stopped, wiped the steam from the mirror once again and looking at his upper lip, repeated the stretches. He thought to himself, this correlates to the way rats control their whiskers, engaging sensory data collection. He repeated the movements again, slower. The tingle came again, stronger. Must be somewhere around the hypothalamus, he thought. He stood up straight and gazed up to his left, remembering Harvard Professor John Mack's research finding: subjects who claim UFO close encounters differ physiologically from control subjects in one objectively measurable way—heightened activity in the hypothalamus. Most claimed some kind of telepathic communication. He could hear Miriam giving several short sighs as she began to stir. He listened for a brief moment, again stretched his upper lip, and then thought to himself, Nah!

By 8:30 that morning human activity resumed in Room L-106. Doctor Klein-Weiss sat at the center workstation. A crowd of students collected around the table. The doctor pulled out a second chair and waved his hand over the keyboard and mouse. "Juwan, you steer. Show us the data you were so excited about. Go ahead, drive this thing."

Juwan's hungover demeanor changed. He came alive, fully charged, as he took control. With several quick movements of the mouse, tables and charts flashed across the two monitors connected to the workstation. Juwan became calmer as he zoomed in on one set of numbers and threw up a graphic representation of the data. "Look at this: Subject Horatio. Series nine. It's as if a switch was flipped. Series three, series four: steady increases in activities correlated to social interaction. But series nine—it's like a capacitor: nothing, nothing, nothing—bang! Then it's full bore from there on. Something has changed categorically." Juwan looked up.

"So, you think maybe this is related to activation of some gene. There are lots of things happening at this time in the subjects. What makes you think this is what you called it—the Enemy gene?"

"The rebel gene." Juwan looked up, shyly, at the tall, gangly individual standing to his right. Milton Wesson was a graduate fellow with a lead role in this study. He had unkempt hair, and a badly pock-marked face, and he always seemed to wear sweaters and knits inappropriate for the season. To be blunt, he held a gravitas inversely proportional to his outward appearance.

"You know," Milton began in a pedantic tone, "there are two other data series that stand out—in my mind—in my mind, anyway. Uhhh. One is series thirteen and the other, uhhh, is series fourteen. Series thirteen is what we studied the last two years—uhhh—communication audible to humans. But series fourteen is new. Theoretically, anyway, it's correlated to hyper-frequency emissions over 20 mega Hertz—signals we can't hear, but Rattus norvegicus can. I theorize that as they enter this stage of development their communication targets change from their sources of food and warmth—parents—to targets with which they seek to avoid conflict or engender cooperation—rounding out the four F's—feeding, fighting, fleeing, and, uhhh, courtship. Imagine a child in your own home. They move from relating to you as child to parent—asymmetrical—and then go out in the world or the playground and relate to their peers as playmate or threat—symmetrical or oppositional."

Doctor K-Dub gazed thoughtfully at the data and from Juwan's face to Milton's. "I can see this might be something.

It's worth pursuing these lines of investigation." He sat in thought for a moment, opening his mouth as if to speak, but saying nothing.

"Wha's it, doc?"

"Juwan, tell me—why is it you called this the rebel gene?"

"Okay. Okay." Juwan breathed deeply. "Think of a child in a family. At first you the parent is to them the source of all things."

Doctor K-Dub interjected, "The source of all good things. The Garden of Delights, Garden of Eden."

"Yes. There is only one category of relationship—child to parent. Then as awareness grows they realize there are also peer relationships—littermates, siblings, playmates. And then degrees of separation—child to teacher, policeman, store clerk—where there is still power differential but not absolute like young child to parent. The first state of submission is like a dog on its back offering its vulnerable underbelly. The second—peer to peer—is like a dog meeting another dog. They meet head-to-head, circle around each other, sniffing butts, taking the measure of each other, and then decide how they'll relate. Dependence then play-fighting. And then learning to recognize threats and respond to them. And then suddenly they get the idea that they need to stand up for themselves. Be the boss. Be in control. They're prepared to stand up face to face—in direct opposition. And then the final step is to see the ultimate safe relationship and flip it. Until that moment, they don't really have that concept available to them. A switch has been flipped. What they've always submitted to, they will now oppose."

A thoughtful Doctor Klein-Weiss asked slowly, "But does it require that there be a peer? If it's really a rebel gene—for example, parent and child on a desert island. There's no peer or degrees of subordination. That would mean that when the gene is triggered, then that child starts to think of the parent as potential enemy instead of as source of all good. That means when that gene is triggered, they wake up one day and see you the parent as the Enemy."

"Yes!" Juwan turned in his chair to face the doctor. "Child suddenly sees parent as enemy; parent has yet to recognize their child is now their enemy." Juwan looked at Doctor K-Dub seriously as scientist to scientist.

Doctor Klein-Weiss looked at Juwan dismissively as teacher to student—even parent to child. He continued to stare for a long moment. "This is the point where HaShem calls out, 'Adam, where are you?' even though he knows exactly where Adam is. And then he asks, 'Who told you you were naked?' which is really asking, 'Why are you trying to hide from me what I gave you in the first place?' Whether the trigger is genetic, behavioral, or even social, this is the challenge or even usurpation."

"Yeah," Milton spoke up. "It's Oedipus. Zeus and Kronos."

"Except Laius and Kronos were not exactly nurturing parents," Doctor K-Dub added. "Oedipus and Zeus had good reason to oppose them. Both were in effect victimized and then reversed their situations—Zeus by might and cunning and Oedipus by fate. But in the analogy of Adam and Eve, it's just a bald-faced betrayal."

"But," Juwan jumped in, "if it's a genetic switch, then Mama rat would detect the change by scent and then they would signal it to others by sound." There was a momentary pause. Juwan continued, "Our subject rats are born thinking—instincting, 'Mama rat will give me whatever's best for me.' And at some point down the line they switch to thinking, 'I need to get mine on my own, whether I take it from my siblings or my parents or someone else in my environment.' "

The crowd around the desk started talking all at once.

Suddenly, Doctor Klein-Weiss waved his hands and called out, "Whoa! Whoa! Whoa!" As the voices died down, he looked around at everyone and then fixed his gaze on Juwan. "Mr. Jeffreys, you have clearly given this idea a lot of thought. But here in this lab, I'll remind you all that we have work to do: to complete the research that has been designed, greenlighted, and funded. So, let's stay focused on that. But I would encourage you as time permits to try to come up with an appropriate experiment design to maybe take the next incremental step toward proving or disproving the elements of your hypothesis. Agreed?"

Doctor Klein-Weiss looked around the room at the growing audience. The crowd started to disburse. Milton patted Juwan awkwardly on the shoulder. As the noise level in the room dropped, Doctor Klein-Weiss felt that he was being watched. From the wall of subject cages behind him, he felt a tingling that somehow told him that several of the twenty-three test subjects were beginning to see him not as a source of all good things but possibly as an opponent to confront or avoid—fight or flee.

The following Thursday, the happy-hour exodus had come and Doctor Klein-Weiss moved Ophelia from her cage to the workstation in the center of the empty lab. It was now October and they were about a third of the way into their adolescent development study. Ophelia was now a month into rat puberty. She would be fully physically mature in two more months. Cognitive and psychological maturity might take another three months. (Of course, physical maturation leads rational decision making by three months.) She would enter menopause by her first birthday. She might live another two years in captivity. If born in the wild, she would be lucky to live out her first year, and as an albino in the wild, she'd have little chance to make it even to maturity.

Doctor Klein-Weiss held her gently. She remained still and silent, anticipating the formality of the brain scan. Once Doctor Klein-Weiss finished with the scan gun and cradled her in both hands, she relaxed. She gave several long squeaks. Doctor Klein-Weiss glanced at the monitor. "Your showing much more self-confidence. Yes, very self-assured. I suppose you're embracing your own identity."

Ophelia stared at the doctor over a long pause and then began bruxing. "You're saying that your anxiety was because you hadn't seen me all day?" She gave a long dainty squeak of affirmation. You said it, not me. Elmo froze momentarily, not sure if he was still pretending or actually communicating, receiving and transmitting thoughts with other brains outside his own.

"We just have to find something for you to do. An activity perfect for Ophelia." She leaned forward and gave a longer squeak. "In due time, hon'. In due time." Dr. Klein-Weiss placed her back in her cage on the right side of the lab. As he approached the bank of cages along the wall, he swore that he was hearing whistles and cat calls from the male fancy rats.

By the end of October, Doctor Klein-Weiss' check-ups with Ophelia would start with her being passive, unreactive—mannequin-like until he completed the brain scan. But she would then become increasingly uneasy—giving long squeaks or grumpy huffing. She no longer focused vaguely on his face but seemed to turn her head to avoid eye contact, wherever his eyes might actually be. And this unease seemed coordinated with the other test subjects becoming more agitated—hissing, chattering, and even screaming by the end of Doctor Klein-Weiss' sessions with Ophelia. Sitting with his back to the other test subjects, it felt like a dozen or so pairs of hostile eyes were focused on his back, a dozen or so sets of claws and teeth wanting to set upon him to get at Ophelia. It was as if the wall behind him were emanating the chatter of a prison cell block except sped up by a factor of three. It felt very tribal, as if he were from the wrong neighborhood—for some reason unacceptable to his twenty-three test subjects and their albino sister.

Adam, why are you hiding? Because somewhere you got the idea that you could be the boss or at least be your own boss. If you weren't trying to hide from my all-seeing eye, I would be guaranteeing you a safe, secure place to sleep and a full stomach every night. In Gan Eden.

As Elmo and Miriam Klein-Weiss walked arm-in-arm from The Taste of Italy on their way to the White Plains Cineplex, Elmo stopped and listened. In the relative quiet of the after-dinner hour, Elmo thought he could make out voices, whispers, high and small. "Do you hear that? It's almost like little voices. No?" He looked around. Along the front of the apartment building, stood several piles of garbage. In the patchy light from the streetlights, Elmo could make out streaks—ghostlike lines that darted so fast they had no dimension. Black or brown streaks running from the side of the building to the garbage piles and back in the blink of an eye. "I don't hear anything," Miriam said, shaking her head. "Come on, we don't want to be late for our movie."

They walked toward the theater. The whispers in Elmo's head seemed to grow smaller and fainter resolving into a single dark emotion. A memory flashed into Elmo's head. It had been almost exactly three years earlier that his daughter, Cyndal, had come home drunk and freshly tattooed and announced to her stunned parents that she wanted to be called from that point forward, "Tatiana."

"Why?" Elmo had asked innocently enough.

Because her girlfriend's boyfriend had introduced them to the wonder of strawberry-infused vodka and convinced her and her friend that it would be great to take a meaningful stand on principle.

"So, why do you want to be called 'Tatiana', dear?" Miriam had asked her daughter patiently.

Out of solidarity with marginalized and unvoiced peoples.

"Do you have any particular marginalized and unvoiced people in mind?" Elmo had quizzed with less compassion.

"Why, all marginalized and unvoiced people," came the principled reply.

"Have you lost sight of the fact that you're named Cyndal after your great grandmother?" Elmo replied, becoming heated. The great-grandmother who miraculously survived Sobibor? Sobibor that was not a work camp, not a concentration camp, but a death camp. What can be more marginalized than to be pulled out of the line for the use of the guards? Who was more unvoiced than Cyndal Klein as she learned the source of the ashes that rained down on the camp day and night?

Cyndal Klein must have asked, Can I obey God without being honest with him? Did she continue to praise as they led her mother away and later when she learned the source of the ashes that fell around the camp every afternoon? And what did she say to HaShem when she realized why the soldiers had spared her life when she arrived? What shock. What lament. How did she even survive? She was beyond marginalized and unvoiced.

Tatiana!

Taking their seats for the movie, Elmo looked seriously at Miriam in the half-light. "Question for you, Miriam: I have a student in the lab promoting the idea of an enemy gene, a rebel gene. I find I keep dismissing the idea. The problem I have with it is that I don't see evidence of it in my own life. I can't get past that. I never opposed my parents or sought to undermine their world. I just don't see it play out in my own life experience."

Miriam looked over at him, dumbfounded. "Seriously?"

Elmo received her silent gaze, and returned it, clueless. "I'm a man of science." He gave his head a muted shake. "I don't see the evidence."

Miriam inclined her head. "You never did or said anything to your parents that made absolutely no sense to them? You never stood up and told them they were dead wrong about anything? And that you were absolutely right?" Miriam shifted in her seat to turn her body toward him. "You never confronted your father and told him that you were opposed to his entire world view?"

Elmo spoke facing the screen, "Not like our daughter did, no." He turned his head toward Miriam. "'I want to be called Tatiana,'" he said with disgust. "Remember that."

"I remember that. But your mother told me about when you said you were done with Hebrew school," Miriam asked, "after just six years. She said you had your heart set on attending a public high school like Bedford Science or City College Math and Science and you felt you needed to go to a public junior high to have a chance to get in. You don't remember anything like that?"

Elmo hung his head. Patrons filled in the seats around them. Advertisements flashed silently on the screen.

Miriam continued now in hushed tones, "Your mother told me once that that was why you and your father stopped talking. And that was why there was such a huge schism between you two."

"No," Elmo said quietly with flagging conviction, "That's just what happens when sons grow up. They just talk about baseball and the weather . . . except I never liked baseball. It never interested me."

"You really don't remember? You must have just blocked out that memory."

Elmo stared into his lap. "Yeah, you're right," Elmo said slowly, quietly. "I did." Miriam could see tears welling in his eyes by the light of Turner Insurance. "I did. I stood in the living room and announced to my father—I stood there and announced to my father that his superstitious idea of education was outright wrong-headed. And I wanted to be a man of modern science."

"And he just accepted this judgment from you?"

"No," Elmo shook his head slowly, a cloud of sadness moving slowly across his face in sepia tones. "No, he did not.

He stood up from his chair and threw down his newspaper. He roared at me like I've never heard him roar. And he said what's peddled as scientific fact today will be out of date in ten years, but what is truth today has always been truth and will always be truth when today's scientists are rotting in their graves." Elmo stared at the screen. "I was so shocked by it . . . by the way he said it . . . I guess I blocked it completely out of my memory." Elmo's eyes teared and his upper lip quivered. "I didn't realize it at the time, but I was telling him his entire worldview—that brought his family out of Germany and Poland and safely to Williamsburg—that all that was garbage, nonsense, and fairy tales. I said that and then I turned and walked out of the living room. He said as I was walking out, 'Be careful what bed you make. You may have to lie in it for all eternity.' I laughed when he said that. Then he went out on the fire escape. We never talked about it again."

Miriam leaned over the armrest, taking his near hand. Elmo leaned in, his face now wet with tears, and looked directly into her eyes. Miriam tilted her head back and whispered into his ear, "*Mayn schatzele*. Has the boy realized that he still needs his father? And that his father still watches and waits?"

Elmo put his other hand on top of their entwined hands. "I think we have to make a trip to Williamsburg."

"You think so?"

"If we don't want to end up isolated by our own flaming swords, fighting off everyone who approaches us, we have to stop and listen. Talk." Elmo took another breath. "We have to start living like we are not enemies."

"I think that's what your father always wanted."

Elmo looked into Mariam's eyes. "And you. You are the joy of my youth, my garden of delights, you are my Gan Eden. I'm done hiding. I'm hoping you are, too." The house lights dropped. The production logo lit up the screen accompanied by a lion's roar.

Pawns

I crossed the park, past the high hurricane fencing of the basketball courts, to the metal tables and chairs set up on the north side of the fountain. Picking a table in clear view of the parking lot, I put my chess board and stadium cushion down on the table and moved the chair nearest the parking lot to the side. Each of the wire mesh chairs was chained to the base of a table and made that dungeon sound, steel on concrete, when you moved them. I put my stadium cushion on the seat of the chair facing the parking lot. As I sat down, the cushion exhaled and so did I. I began to set up the board, wiping each piece with my t-shirt and positioning them on the board: kings, queens, rooks, bishops, knights, and pawns. I paused over one black pawn with a long nick in his top knob, exposing a weathered sliver of bare wood. I placed him in front of my queen's rook. With the board set, I sat back and scanned the parking lot for my son Gerry's blue van.

A radio announcer could be heard, "Join Rick Rush tonight at 8:00 PM when he talks with Buzz Aldrin to commemorate the anniversary of the Apollo 11 moon landing—

the day that America conquered the moon!" Someone changed the station. It paused on a Latin station—"Dura, dura, dura"—and then slid to sixties classics: the tail end of "Georgie Girl" and then the beginning of "Incense and Peppermints."

The house was up, I was aware of an electricity of movement, a muted buzz. Sliding out from under my covers, I glanced across the room at Jake's side of the room. On the wall above his bed hung his framed high-school diploma—Class of '67—and his senior prom photo with Cindy Skulnik. It had been like living with a ghost for the past year. His headboard with the built-in bookcase held almost a year's worth of Life Magazines carefully curated by our mother who saved them all for Jake to read when he returned home. The covers told the story of the year: hippies, moon landing, Norman Mailer (?), astronaut, off to the moon, the faces of our dead, American flag on the moon, more astronauts, more moon photos, more soldiers, science, and something about sex. I thought, Jake'll be really surprised when he reads about everything that's happened since he's been away. For the past year, our mother had come into the room repeatedly just to stand over the foot of Jake's bed clutching the cross that hung around her neck. Our father had taken to walking slowly into the room, pursing his lips, usually looking down at the floor, in constant motion, occasionally scanning the walls of the room as if he'd forgotten something. This morning, I shuffled across the floor in my footsy pajamas drawn by the unsettled sounds of the house.

Peering out the door and down the hall, I could see the yellow glow of the kitchen. Already a creature of habit, I had to first shuffle across the living room and sit down cross-legged in front of the TV, pressing my nose and forehead up against the convex screen. Pulling the knob out, I watched patiently for the first dot to appear in the center of the screen. Ten, twenty, thirty seconds passed before the first grey-white dot appeared in the center of the screen, another ten before that seminal point of light began to spread outward. This morning no one chided me, "Sit back! You'll ruin your eyes!" I slid back to arm's length from the TV. I soon saw snow and static, realized that there was nothing to watch yet, confirming that this morning was starting strangely, not like other mornings.

I got up, left the snowy screen, and padded quietly down the hall toward the harsh yellow light. Squinting as I approached the kitchen doorway, I peered around the doorjamb. My father, in his bathrobe, pajamas, and slippers, sat on one of the kitchen chairs, his back to the doorway, tapping one slippered foot nervously like some jittery jazz drummer on Joey Bishop or Dick Cavett. The long, spiral cord of the black wall-phone was draped from the wall-mount over his shoulder. He had the chair pulled out from the table at an angle. He smoked, repeatedly flicking ashes toward the ashtray on the kitchen table, often missing. Agitated, he swept them off nervously with the side of his hand holding the lit cigarette, scattering more ashes with each wave of his hand, perpetuating the cycle. My mother observed and for once said nothing. With a serious look that I had only seen once before, she turned from the table. A shadow of a smile crossed her face as she glanced at me, and she turned to the stove and counter. She moved as if scripted, following an order of service, completing the motions she had executed thousands of times before, seeming to know that at this moment they held unique import: taking the coffee can from the shelf next to the stove, reaching into the can making that scoop sound and depositing the grounds into the basket inside the percolator that sat in its proper place on the left rear burner of the stove, and again into can, "Hooh," and then to the percolator basket, "Haah," followed by the metallic sound of the lid being replaced on the percolator, returning the coffee can to its shelf, turning on the gas burner, "Whooshh," first for the coffee and then for the cast iron skillet on the right front burner. Moving down the counter, she retrieved two slices of Wonder Bread. Into the toaster and down with a firm push of the handle. Then back to the skillet where she would add one by one strips of bacon into the sizzle.

Finally, my father spoke. "So, he's stable." He cleared his throat. "Stable." He seemed to be eating his lower lip between words. "On his way to Okinawa." He looked up at my mother, as if to see that she understood the significance of the words. Their eyes met. Their expressions gave no sign of relief, not following any familiar pattern of communication. As my eyes adjusted to the overhead light, I realized that this was a moment when somehow lives would turn. This was a family moon landing—maybe bigger. I became aware that information was flowing around the room without words, with glances and nods. I knew instinctively it was a moment I needed to remember. My mother was performing a sacrament that attested to continuation of life. My father was in the role of Egyptian father who realized too late that he'd failed to mark his lintel and door posts the way those peculiar Hebrews did, only in this case, the Dark Angel had not taken his full measure, a check swing with the old scythe. "Thank you. Thank you, sir."

I could hear bits of the thin voice on the other end of the line: "You don't have to call me 'sir.' You're not in the army." I would learn later that my father had never been in the army—or any other armed service. He hadn't passed the physical. He'd served in the Office of Civil Defense—as a kind of home-front hall monitor, enforcing blackout orders and keeping an eye out for suspicious characters skulking around our seaports.

My father finally spoke, straightening up in his chair, "Okay, thank you." Shaking, he rose from the chair, reached with the receiver to place it in its cradle on the wall, and sat back down with a jerky quickness not customary to him.

He looked over at my mother and then down at me. "Shermy, you know Jake's over there fighting the war, right? You understand that, right?"

I nodded as I absently sucked on the knuckle of my index finger.

"Honey," my mother said to my father.

He nodded to her and looked back at me. "Your brother was in a big battle last night. He was in an armored personnel carrier and they took incoming rounds."

"Honey."

"He was hurt pretty badly, but he's ok now. He's in a hospital. They'll be fixing him up, OK? He's going to be coming home when he's, when he's well enough." He looked at me for recognition. I nodded. He looked back at my mother and continued, "He's being moved from the field hospital to, to Okinawa. Then when he's ready to travel, he'll come back to the states. To San Diego and then probably home for good."

"How long before he gets home?"

"It'll be weeks. But he'll be in good hands."

"Where's he hurt, can you say?" She nodded toward me.

Father looked down at me, and then said to my mother, "Left leg. Plus some shrapnel . . . in his thigh and . . . buttocks. They're gonna to try to save his right hand." They looked at each other seriously. The sound from the skillet had reached a high hiss and smoke started to rise. My mother turned to slide bacon out of the pan onto a plate. She then deftly wrapped a dishtowel around the skillet handle, lifted the sizzling skillet off the burner, and carried it over to the sink. There she appeared to pour the sizzle sound along with hot bacon grease into an empty jar, and then efficiently returning to the stovetop, she slid several more strips of bacon into the pan, the sizzle returning as the bacon fat began to liquify. My father's cigarette had burned itself out. He stubbed it out in the ashtray and reached for his pack of cigarettes, patting his chest pocket and then seeing it on the table in front of him.

"What's going on?" came Audrey's voice from the doorway. My two sisters were now peering into the kitchen. They were both closer in age to Jake than they were to me, Audrey ninth grade, Patty sixth.

My mother gave me a strip of unusually crispy bacon and I walked out of the kitchen. Behind me, my sisters began talking briskly about what it meant, whose brothers were heroes, who received metals, who came home and whose families were met at the airport by color guards with caskets draped with flags.

Bacon told me life would go on. I pondered whether Jake was yet a full-fledged hero, what praise he would receive from generals and senators. Whether the President would call from the White House. Whether he would have plaques with his name on them. I imagined him home again in a few weeks, probably going back to his regular routine.

By the time I reached the living room, my bacon was gone. The Indian chief test pattern was on the screen counting down—5, 4, 3, 2, 1. "Our broadcast day has begun." The Indian head told me it was on channel 4. I turned the knob two clicks this way.

The screen flashed to a picture of a heart wrapped in what appeared to be barbed wire. A note or two of instrumental music and a thin choir chimed, "O, sacred heart, our home lies deep in thee." And then as if that was introduction enough, a deep solemn voice began, "Hail, Mary, full of grace, the Lord is with thee. Blessed art thou amongst women and blessed is the fruit of thy womb, Jesus. Holy Mary, mother of God, pray for us sinners, now and at the hour of our death. Amen." The voice repeated it over and over again, but there was nothing better on at this hour. Even so, this was the right channel to be on for the next quarter hour. Davy and Goliath would come on. And then Gumby. Commercials would play between shows: Choo-Choo Charlie who used Good 'n' Plenty candy to make his train run. Quisp, the pink space man, and Quake, the miner. When Gumby was half-over, they showed the Marvel the Mustang commercial—"No winding, no batteries. Marvel the Mustang, do we love you?" As the Marvel jingle played, I looked around to see if my mother or father might be within earshot. Usually before Gumby was over, my sisters went off to school. After Gumby, the commercial played for Palisades Park—"Come on over!" And then the Chock Full o' Nuts song:

Chock Full o' Nuts is the heav-enly coffee, heav-enly coffee.

Better coffee a Rockefeller's mon-ey can't buy.

And then the CBS Morning News would come on and it was time to go five clicks that way past WABD-5, the Dumont Television Network, to WABC TV-7. TV-7 was always changing what it showed, but it was better than CBS Morning News. Plus, TV-7 would go right to Captain Kangaroo. Captain of what? Certainly no kangaroo. And no one—no one—believed he could fall for that ping-pong-ball bit even one more time. He strained credulity. I wondered how many medals Jake would have when he got home. People were dying every day. They reported it every night—the body count—always more of them than us, so that's good. That's good. And every night, napalm. *They* don't have napalm; we have lots of napalm. Also good, right? Jake was sure to come home a hero with a bunch of medals. In a couple weeks.

Still no sign of Gerry. Sometimes he runs a little late. He was never one to be punctual, even as a child. I have nowhere to be. The light breeze breathed through the tree branches overhead and dappled sun played on the table and chairs. The wind picked up again and someone was playing Beach Boys: "God only knows what I'd be without you. God only knows what —." From nearby on the basketball courts, Run DMC cut in for four beats, only to be immediately drowned out by the blare of an ambulance siren speeding by the far side of the park. The sounds of the life of the city continued to pick up as the sun climbed overhead.

Jake finally came home eight weeks later. He was missing half of his left leg, and his right hand was blue where they had taken skin from the back of his thigh and attached it over severe burns on his right forearm and hand. After about a week, he let me touch the blue part of his hand. He had to learn to walk on crutches and then months later, he had to learn to walk with a prosthetic foot. He also had to go through several more operations and physical therapy to try to get the full use of his hand back. He did come home with three medals. He showed me once where he kept them next to his socks.

That was the year of night terrors. Flashbacks. But Jake said very little about them. About a year later, he moved into a halfway house for disabled veterans. I heard clinical talk about his isolating and using marijuana. Some said it would help him with his flashbacks, but it still wasn't legal, and it wasn't clear that it really helped enough.

Time passed. I went away to Fordham. I was in a dorm on a hall phone when I took the last call about Jake.

I stared at the chessboard. The four central pawns, black and white, kings' and queens' pawns, were usually the first thrown into the fray and the most likely to be the first off the board. The scarred pawn sat to the far right fronting a rook. If only Jake had been lucky enough to be that rook's pawn and not one of the central pawns. Then he might have been on the board until the end of the game.

And I remembered when our own midnight call came. It was after we had returned home from a Superbowl party—Superbowl XLVII, the "Harbowl," brothers Jim and John

Harbaugh coaching the opposing teams. It was 2:00 AM before we got to bed. And then the phone rang at 3:21, just when we'd dozed off. When we recognized it was the phone ringing, that sick feeling set in. Darlene was a wreck, almost incomprehensible. "Why did you let him go? How could you let them take my baby? What does this accomplish? Who benefits from this? No one! No one!" She disappeared into the bathroom and I could hear running water. And occasionally, over the running water, I could hear through her sobbing, "I can't. I can't lose him. I can't." She later apologized, but, of course, no apology was necessary. I just felt powerless. And guilty. Like my own father, I had never actually served. There had been no draft as I came of age, no hard decisions, no answering the call of duty. It felt as though our Gerry had been taken in my place, for my failure to offer myself up.

A blue van pulled into the parking lot. Gerry parked and then waved from the driver's seat. He disappeared into the back of the van. The rear passenger-side door slid open. An electric lift folded down. Gerry rolled onto the lift platform and worked the controls lowering it to the pavement. He deftly exited the lift, secured the van, and made his way from the parking lot to the concrete pavement of the park and over to our table.

We hugged. He apologized for being late. He'd had a last-minute discipline problem with one of the at-risk teens that he worked with as a reform-school guidance counselor.

We turned our attention to the chessboard. We played quickly, knowing each other's tendencies, having met almost every Saturday for the better part of the past year. "Are you still enjoying your work . . . at the juvy place?"

"I am." Gerry looked up from the board to smile at me. I caught a glimpse of the ten-year-old boy I'd first taught to play chess. "But I'd rather be back with my unit." Back to grown-up Gerry.

"You'd still rather be fighting a war," I gave a little laugh, "than working with high school kids?"

"That doesn't sound right, does it. But I've been in that job for . . . fifteen months? I've had my own adjustments. I still don't really know *how* to do my job all that well. But the thing is that when I was in the service, I was with a group of guys who all knew what our mission was, and we were all there for the mission we had been trained for. And we had each other's backs. We were tight." Gerry looked at me. "Now I'm working with a bunch of kids who, when they first arrive, they just see me as The Man, part of the system that's coming down on them. They don't understand that I'm really there to help them. They're suspicious of me. My supervisor, he says that once I see a few kids through from arrival to departure, I'll start to understand how to build rapport, build relationships, see the results of my work. I'll earn a reputation, and if kids learn that I actually help them in real ways, then it will be good. That's when the satisfaction will come. So he says." While speaking, Gerry has taken my king's pawn with his king's knight.

"I guess I see." I slid my queen's bishop out to the king's file.

"It'll take a little time." Gerry captured the pawn in front of my king's bishop. Suddenly, he's threatening both my rook and my queen. Apparently, I haven't been focusing on the game.

I moved my queen out of harm's way. "I was thinking about your uncle. He was like your king's pawn there. He had barely been in-country before he became a casualty. And he never really had a chance after that. I kinda wish he could have been like one of your rooks' pawns and had a good long run, maybe even be there for the duration of the game. You know? I just wish he had a chance. . . He never chose to be a hero."

Gerry captured my rook. I took the opportunity to execute a queenside castle and move my king further from the action.

"Presidents and senators send young men and women to fight and die. Whether they're wisemen or fools, I think you could always argue. But that's out of our hands." Gerry brought out his queen diagonally. "And life's not fair. You can count on that. Check."

I moved my king to the left out of danger.

Gerry continued. "But given that life's unfair, every man, every person, has to decide how to respond to their unfair situation as best they can. Maybe you never got to talk to any of the men Jake served with. Your folks probably got a letter from his commanding officer telling you a little bit about what happened." Gerry leaned forward. "But every time we go out on patrol, every single man in that unit is resolved that if at all possible, they're going to make sure every man comes back alive. And if that's not possible, they're resolved that if necessary, they'll do what it takes to bring home every other man in their unit, even if it means they don't come back. Because they know that every other man there would do the same for them." Gerry took my king's knight with his bishop. "And maybe things were different fifty years ago—with the draft and all. But, how does it go? The highest love is to give up yourself for your brother? Did you ever think that maybe Jake was thinking that every time he went out on patrol, yes he was not only trying to stay alive, but even more he was trying to make sure that no one else in his unit failed to come back, and that beyond that, maybe he was thinking that he was doing what he was doing so that you wouldn't have to do it when you were eighteen?" For the moment, there seemed to be a pause in Gerry's relentless attack. He seemed to be pondering. Without looking up from the board, he said, "How do I get Nana to stop calling me Jake?"

"Like you said, life's not fair."

He seemed at odds about how to continue the attack. "But you know what I'm really wondering?"

"What?"

"You seem to have this sense of tragedy about Jake not having choices, not choosing to do anything heroic. But we all have choices. So this lack of heroism that seems to be bothering you—was it lacking in Jake? Or in you?"

Sailing the Etta Lee

The mailbox still says "Carl and Etta Ivers." Etta's voice still answers the calls that Carl doesn't want to pick up. The Car-Bargains truck had already picked up Etta's hot pink VW Beetle convertible, even though she'd passed less than ten days ago. The Ivers have been in Orchid Beach for nearly three months already, but Carl never took the steps to sell his own truck as they had planned. He couldn't quite make that call.

This move was supposed to be for Etta's health—just what she needed—to Indian River County, Florida, from Schroon Lake, Essex County, New York.

The phone rings, rings, rings. "We're the Ivers'. Leave a message." The machine beeps and then another message is left in a sing-song saccharine-sweet voice full of pale sympathy. "Hi, Carl! I hope you're doing okay today. Let me know if I can help. 954-!" He was past being interested. And again, the answering message, the beep, and another message, "Carl, hun, I was pedaling my little bicycle by your house this morning and I saw that the meal I left yesterday on your front step was still sitting there. Thank Gawd I put it in a cold pack! But you might want to bring that inside, hun. See ya re-e-eal soon!" Carl rolled his eyes and got up from his Lazy Boy leaving his oatmeal untouched along with the OJ, an empty Old-Fashioned glass, and a forty-five automatic. He walked reluctantly to the front door, opened it and looked at the stack of casseroles and packaged meals that sat on his front step. Each one had hand-written heating instructions decorated with hearts and smileys. He took a step and straddled the stack and then bent over to move them one by one from his front step into his foyer. As he reached down to grab the next casserole dish, he heard, "Morning, Carl!" Still bent over, Carl looked up and out toward the street to see Jenelle Trollope in her apricot spandex unitard with her wrist and ankle weights speed-walking with exaggerated steps. She executed a quick loop in front of the house. "Keeping active!" She forced a laugh. "And flexible! See-e-e-e ya-a-a-a!" And she was gone.

Carl dropped his head and grasped the last of the cold-packed meals. He stood up straight and stepped back inside, pulling the door shut behind him. He then carried the meals one or two at a time from the foyer to the kitchen, where he piled them on top of several more days of meals. The doorbell rang. Carl walked toward the foyer and then turned abruptly to enter the powder room. He closed the door behind him. The loud hum of the fan drowned out all other sounds. He leaned on the pedestal sink and looked into the mirror. He saw a sad out-of-place old man with a weeks' worth of beard growth in a silk hibiscus-print shirt, and behind that man he saw the mirror image of a framed panoramic photo of Carl and Etta Ivers and a half dozen of their closest friends on a frozen Schroon Lake. Etta was in her black-and-red snow suit having just gotten off her Ski-

Doo Mach Z. Carl had driven his Yamaha four-by-four to haul their bob-house—their portable ice-fishing shack—onto the ice. The Jansens on their new Polaris had pulled up right behind Etta. Off to the side sat Boo—who never looked happy about anything—on the police snow machine. Someone from the Ice Festival Committee had captured the moment as Etta dismounted her snowmobile, removed her helmet, shook out her hair, and then leaned forward to slap Carl's snow-suited butt. It looked like a beer commercial—a bunch of friends in their prime loving life. The January afternoon sun was reaching the point where it seemed to cut right through the pines, setting all the buildings along that edge of the lake ablaze.

Carl stood up straight, looked himself in the mirror, and dried his eyes. They should have known, he thought to himself, they should have known that such a moment could never be matched again—a moment when everything was just right. He grabbed the photo and returned to the kitchen where he sat down at the breakfast table with a pad of paper and began to sketch out plans for a bob-house.

A bob-house is not just an ice fishing hut. A bob-house is a portable home away from home. An ephemeral mancave, a pleasure palace whose appearance is heralded by the nearly silent singing of the lake's freezing surface. It appears when conditions are just right, and then it disappears just as mysteriously like the morning mist sometime before ice-out—when the lake is once again cleared of ice. A bob-house is a celebration of winter that provides warmth and all the conveniences of home plus an auger hole for ice access. This miracle of mancraft appears only for a season—for a few weeks or weekends, depending on the occupants' depth of devotion to the gods of ice sport. A focal point for people who don't just brave the outdoors in winter but thrive in it. A bob-house represented everything that was missing in Carl's life at that moment. Everything he could cast his eye on was there for Etta, but there was no Etta. He set about doing what was familiar—designing, building, lighting up that part of his mind that never seemed to tire and using those leathery hands driven by muscle memory to do what he knew and loved. Because this was what Carl does.

When Carl's fever passed, he had drawn up a scale drawing and parts list for the most beautiful bob-house anyone had ever imagined. It was designed to fit on a standard long utility trailer. It wasn't the standard design that most harried men slap together based on one sheet of plywood per end and two sheets per side, top, and bottom. Carl was a craftsman, and this was his masterpiece of a bob-house. It used golden rectangle ratios. It specified the best materials. It would be equipped with propane, passive solar, and high-capacity battery stores. It had a heavy-duty tow yoke on the front and a standard 36-inch-wide steel fire door on the back. It would be finished with an aluminum sheet-metal skin. It would contain a propane stove, a microwave, and a macerating toilet. It would have four-by-six skids to stand up to the full weight being dragged across the frozen ice. It would be the Aristotelian ideal of a bob-house made manifest. Carl could just buy a state-of-the-art RV. This was Florida. But as if in a trance he was already on the phone with the home store ordering everything on his parts list and having it delivered to his home address, Orchid Beach, Florida. Because Carl had to build this bob-house now.

The order went smoothly item by item until Carl reached the last item on his list. "I need a 48-foot roll of 49-inch ought-point-ought-three-inch aluminum sheet."

"What color? The only color we have in stock is opaluminum."

"Okay," Carl sighed, "opaluminum."

Carl went out to the garage, which was still half full of boxes that hadn't been unpacked from their move. He slid several wardrobe boxes and rolled his toolbox to the front of the garage. He rolled out his portable chop saw. His standing chop saw had been given away when they moved. He opened his tool chest and pulled out his circular saw. He pulled out his sawhorse brackets and laid them out where they would be needed.

Carl pulled his pickup out to the curb and parked it in front of the house. No sooner had he parked than the home store delivery truck arrived with his order. "You guys are fast! I like it."

"When we get an order like that, we mo-o-o-ove!" The delivery driver actually spoke with a native Florida drawl and moved with a slow shambling gate, sliding out of his cab and lowering the forklift from the back of the truck. But he made quick work of dropping the three pallets of lumber and building materials. Carl signed for the order and waved as the driver climbed into his cab.

The ladies in the neighborhood were already buzzing around. In this neighborhood, garage doors opened and garage doors closed. They seldom stayed open. And now in their midst an unattached man was preparing to do physical labor in his driveway. It was catnip!

The women started swarming like bees. Carl felt like a space-coast Noah.

"What ya building, Carl?"

"A bob-house."

"What's that?"

"Look it up."

"It's an ice-fishing house?"

"Where are you going ice-fishing around here?"

The chatter snowballed until voices seemed disembodied and non-directional. "He's building an ice-fishing shack!" "He's gone bonkers." "He's grieving. He's still in the denial stage." "He needs someone to clear his head—I could help with that."

As Carl laid down the six-and-a-half by seventeen-foot foundation of an ice-fishing Xanadu in his driveway, it became clear that Carl, like Nehemiah on his wall, could not be dragged from his task at hand by any offered distraction. The lady cloud began to dissipate. By evening, Carl had finished framing and sheathing the bob-house. Passersby were now few and far between. Mildred Barkley from three houses down came by drinking a glass of wine.

"You ready for a beer, Carl—want to share a bottle of wine?"

"What?" Carl turned and looked. "No, Mildred. I got work to do."

"God loves a workin' man," she said under her breath. "You sure? It doesn't have to be a drink. Take a break. Freshen up. I'll get you a hot shower." She smiled over her wine glass.

"No, Mildred."

Mildred smiled, tilted her head. "Okay, . . . just remember, I'm only a couple doors down . . . if you get a hankering."

"No, Mildred." He answered without looking away from his work.

Carl worked until the early hours. The omnipresent white noise of air conditioning filled in the tenor range permeating the neighborhood. The tree frogs and cicadas contributed their soprano notes floating above other sounds. And the small bass and percussion of one man hammering, sawing, and ratcheting drove the driving rhythm of work throughout the night. After cutting and applying the opaluminum to the outside of the bob-house and mounting the solar panels to the roof and wiring them into the electrical system, Carl looked around and smiled. It was very good. Sixteen hours earlier his driveway had been empty, except for three pallets of building supplies next to the curb. It now contained just a small pile of odds and ends and trimmings along the curb and one glorious opaluminum bob-house dramatically lit by the Ivers' external garage lights. Carl swept up the scraps and dumped them into his bin. He turned off the work lights inside and alongside the bob-house. He climbed into his truck and drove away.

By sunrise, he was pulling into Winston's Salvage-and-Restoration Yard in Ocala. The owner of the yard stepped to the office door, locked eyes with Carl, exchanged a nod, and went back inside his office—completing the necessary manspeak. In a half hour or so, Carl appeared pushing a dolly loaded with a three-foot nautical figurehead—a buxom gold-leaf-haired mermaid shouting madly into the maelstrom. Leaving it outside the office, he went inside, transacted his business, emerged to load the figurehead into the back of his truck, and headed back down the highway.

Well before noon, Carl was backing into his driveway to unload the figurehead. With a couple sawhorses and a few scrap pieces of two-by-four for stabilization, he adroitly mounted the carved figure to the yoke end of the bob-house. With a few adroit pencil marks on the opaluminum for reference, he applied adhesive lettering—Gothic font—beneath the figurehead: Etta Lee. Carl went back into the house and emerged again with the photo from the powder room. Sitting down in one of his deluxe camp chairs, he held the photo in both hands and felt exhaustion overcome him like a sea wave. He slumped down in the chair and continuing to gaze at the photo, repeatedly tracing the figures in the frame. What Carl did not know was that he was casting an emotionally-fed electromagnetic anchor. And his bob-house had been pulled from his driveway in Orchid Beach, Florida, and slung from the year in which he had begun his day.

Carl was roused from his trance by the sound of wooden skids scraping on ice. He got up from his chair, walked to the door, and opened it only to find a blizzard raging outside. Carl tried to lean out to gauge the storm better and was sucked out and thrown twenty feet across the ice. From where he landed, he realized that what had appeared to be a winter squall from inside the bob-house had actually been a pristine wintry calm in which only the bob-house had been spinning. Carl jumped up, brushed off his silk floral shirt, and ran back to the open door. Shivering, he hastily shut himself inside and turned on his heaters. He sat confused. A knock came at the door. Opening the door, Carl stood face to face with a younger, taller, apparently more vital version of himself. "Howdy, neighbor!"

Young Carl stood properly dressed for the cold. His 4x4 was parked behind him and in the cargo rack sat Mookie, Carl's golden retriever. The dog jumped from the 4x4 and approached slowly, looking and sniffing, looking back and forth from Elder to Younger. Standing just behind the Younger, a change came over the dog—a bolt of recognition and he began wagging his fluffy tail wildly and dashed back and forth between Elder and Younger, falling at the feet of Elder and then jumping up on both men. Carl the Younger spoke up apologetically, “Sorry. He seems to like you, man.” He grabbed Mookie’s collar and pulled him out of the bob-house. “But you seem okay with it.”

“Yeah, I love dogs.”

“I stopped by to say hi. Your bob-house just showed up suddenly. I didn’t see you hauling it out. Your house didn’t look familiar—man, it’s ... it’s ... de-luxe.” Young Carl paused to touch the opaluminum skin. “But *you* look strangely familiar. Have you been here before? Do I know you? Don’t mean to be nosy. But I represent the festival committee.” He pulled a lanyard out of the collar of his snow suit.

“I think you might know me indirectly.”

“If you haven’t been here before, I should let you know that there’s a festival tent over there,” he pointed across the ice toward a cluster of tents and folding pavilions. “If you want to register for the fishing derby—over there. And if you need anything—first aid, a hot drink, a light for your stove, anything.”

“Thanks, dude.” The Elder stood shivering, and realizing he was freezing, he shut the door.

Inside, Carl sat down, rubbing his shoulders and arms for warmth. He made a quick circuit around the cabin interior. He checked to see that his heating was set and operating properly. He pulled his old snow suit out of the closet and climbed into it. If anything, it was now too big for him in the shoulders and too long in the legs. He had lost two or three inches in height and maybe fifteen pounds of muscle mass in general since he had been that man who represented the festival committee. He picked up the picture that he’d taken from the powder room. Looking it over, he marveled that he was actually there in that picture in that place with those people. He felt transported, as though the photo now held greater meaning than when he had taken it from the powder room. There was Etta sitting on her snowmobile and Carl having just climbed off his 4-wheeler. He was walking away from Etta. Right behind Etta were the Jansens, both on their new Polaris. Off to the side was Officer Boo sitting on the police snow machine. And behind them all was the pop-up pavilion of the festival organizers with some unidentifiable volunteer working the table helping someone register, head down immersed in the paperwork.

The officer was Ray *Bukoski*, a teddy bear of a cop. People just called him Boo, but never to his face. He was old for a police officer—for one that didn't get promoted to captain or chief. And there was a special sadness in his face as he looked side-eyed at the camera, like this festivity was not for him. Yes, he had lost his wife to a drunk driver the previous year. All these happy faces, and then Boo staring down at the Jansen's registration tags. You dedicate your life to protecting people and they go ahead and do stupid things that shouldn't have to happen. Dumb kids drinking and joyriding. People up from the City in their ridiculously large vacation homes and over-sized SUVs—no regard for the locals. Carl heard all the side chatter that had been a part of that season come flooding back in an instant.

And the unidentifiable person working the festival pavilion when that picture was taken was Becky Weliver. Becky Weliver. After this picture was taken, Etta and the Jansens would head off down the length of the lake opening up their machines full throttle. They'd probably take four or five passes running the full length of the lake before they were done, and then they'd go into the Jansens' bob-house for some hot refreshment. As soon as the three of them took off, backs to the pavilion, Becky Weliver would come out from under the flap and walk by Carl, staring brazenly at him, and continue crossing to the near side of the lake to the Weliver's boat house. She would enter by the door facing their house. Carl would follow a couple minutes later trying not to draw attention and enter through the far door.

The vicious talk around town was that Becky's marriage had fallen apart in everything but legal status three or four years ago. She was said to entertain herself with all comers—another vicious rumor probably started by her husband, Nat Weliver. The town generally believed there to be some amount of truth to it, and her response to the talk seemed to be to stare it down from whence it came. "And just what would you do?" was the response attributed to her, "What would you do with that sad example of a man that I have to go home to?" Two toxic people who both seemed to want nothing more than to deliver a fatal blow to the other. It was further rumored that she had constructed a comfortable love nest inside the Weliver's boat house—inside the winter occupant, their thirty-foot Sea-Ray cabin cruiser.

This snow-devil of memories came spinning back to Carl inside the Etta Lee. He placed the picture face down on the table and stepped out of his Xanadu and into the cold whipping winds. He had fueled his flight with heart-felt nostalgia and morose disappointment at how his last year had gone. Suddenly he felt a deeper regret recognizing a spreading crater of damage. This had not only been part of the happiest season of their lives, this winter in particular had been the end of that season. In fact, when Carl hauled his bob-house off the ice and the Ivers returned full-time to their house on Glendennis Street, Etta would seem closed and distant, like a pall had come over their marriage. She seemed from that time on to gradually make herself unnecessarily busy. And falsely cheerful. Taking the long view, there would be no more children for the Ivers. They'd only have the one. Carl had actually hoped that when they retired to Orchid Beach, they might rekindle some of what they had once had. Orchid Beach would be too late for any more kids, but Carl had hoped for a return of the tenderness, the intimacy. Maybe the platonic roommate dynamic could thaw.

Closing the door behind him, he felt the warmth draining from the core of his body and then his heart shifting gears, furiously pumping blood to his core and essential organs. This was the kind of circumstance that causes men his age to drop dead shoveling show. Temperature of face, hands, and feet began to drop. He spotted the festival pavilion and headed out in that general direction. To his right, he saw three snowmobilers on two machines speeding off down the lake and recognized them right way as Etta's Ski-Doo and the Jansens' new Polaris. Looking up he saw the Younger and Boo standing by their individual machines. Boo was starting his machine up and began what seemed like a routine patrol around the various bob-houses and clusters of men and women around the near side of the lake.

Becky Weliver stood up and walked out from under the pavilion and—could this be the very moment? Yes, the festival volunteer who had snapped the photo that now sat face down in the Elder's bob-house stood taking one more picture of the Younger standing by his four-wheeler and spun around to catch one more image of Officer Boo driving his machine standing up scanning the lake. She then walked into the unattended festival popup canopy.

The Elder knew what the Younger would do next. He would start walking straight out across the frozen lake describing an oblique circuit that would only point directly at the Weliver's boat house as it neared its end.

In similar fashion, the Elder began a path that at first headed toward the festival canopy pavilion half a mile away. As he made his way down the lake, he gradually veered more and more in the direction of the boat house. By the time the Younger's destination had become clear, the Elder was ten feet behind him. Already winded from trudging through the four-to-six inches of snow, he managed one last sprint to catch the Younger before he reached the boat house.

Hearing the swishing of gore-tex thighs behind him, the Younger turned and saw an older version of himself huffing and puffing, red in the face, about to launch himself into the air. The Younger put out two arms and deflected him. The Elder fell at the Younger's feet.

"What are you doing old man?"

The Elder swung one arm and was able to grab a snow boot. As the Younger fell backward in the snow, the Elder growled, "I'm trying to stop you from making the biggest mistake of our life." Both men were now doing swim strokes in the snow, one trying to gain purchase on the other man, the other seeking to skate free. "Etta doesn't deserve this." He could feel the boot coming free of the foot. "She won't ever get over it." He hurled the free boot at the other's head. "Our marriage will die a silent death," he whispered hoarsely. He was now lying on his stomach and staring up at the other man, who himself was lying on his back, barely raising his head. "And over the next twenty years, so will both of you."

"What are you babbling about? What are you, some kind of psycho?" They had ceased struggling.

"I'm your conscience." The Elder raised up on his elbows. "And I have the same snow suit you do."

"Old man, you're nuts! You're not making any sense!"

"I may be," he conceded, "but you're the one who's doing the stupidest thing you'll do your whole life. Just use your brain. And not this," he said lunging to reach the Younger's crotch with a gloved left hook.

The Younger groaned and bent over, grabbing the other man's arm and flinging it away. In the same motion, he rolled over on his side rocking in the fetal position. Between moans, he said, "Gimme my boot."

The Elder got to his feet. "Not today, Carl!" he shouted nodding toward the boat house.

The other man sat up with a look of murderous exposure.

The Elder continued, "You're not going in there tonight. You're not going in there ever. Use your head." He extended a hand to his Younger self.

Staring coldly at the older man, the Younger shook his head and growled, "You are certifiable, mister. One thing is sure, I can't go in there now *discreetly*. So, I guess the only thing to do is—uh—regroup. Just try another time."

"The only thing to do is think long and hard." The Elder turned and began walking back to Xanadu. He called back one more time, "Think long and hard! We both really want the same thing."

Both Carls watched as three snowmobilers returned to the area around the pavilion, turned their machines around, and headed back down the length of the lake. The Younger returned to the pavilion, and as he did so, Officer Boo approached him.

The Elder returned to the Etta Lee and climbed inside. He removed his snow suit. Underneath, his shirt and pants were soaked with sweat. He pulled out a dry change of clothes and gave some thought to a nice warm beverage. A sense of peace descended on the Etta Lee. Carl picked up the photo again.

Thirty minutes later, a knock was heard. Carl opened the door to find Officer Boo with his sorry-to-have-to-tell-you-this face. "Mister, uh . . . , Mister?" Boo stammered. "We need to talk."

"Well come right in, please!"

Boo, slightly taken aback, smiled. "Why, sure, don't mind if I do." He entered with the circumspection of someone entering a palace.

"Please have a seat."

"Thank you." Boo felt the same sense of peace. He smiled and the familiar deep lines eased. "Well, you see, I talked to Carl Ivers." Boo stared at Carl. "You know Carl Ivers." He continued staring at Carl. Something was clearly playing through his mind that he could not put into words. "Well, Carl said that whatever went on between you two a little earlier was quote unquote nothing. In his words, everything's cool." Boo shifted in his seat. "And yes, if there were no other witnesses, I could accept that and sweep it all under the rug." Boo looked serious. "But Becky Weliver—you know Becky Weliver—Becky Weliver hunted me down and said she witnessed an assault. An eyewitness to an assault. I have no choice but to treat that as criminal activity. I can no longer make it go away. She's on record saying she witnessed a crime. And she fingered you as the perpetrator." Boo stared sadly at Carl.

Carl smiled. "And who did she say was the perpetrator?"

"Uh," Boo paused momentarily. "Her exact words were, 'That crazy old man in that bob-house with the angry witch hung on the one end.' "

Carl continued to smile to himself. "Officer Boo-."

"Bukaski."

"Officer Bukaski, if you could be so gracious as to give me a couple minutes to enjoy this peaceful moment before you have to arrest me, I would be forever in your debt."

Boo nodded. "Go ahead, take your minute."

Carl held the picture frame in two hands, staring down at it until he gradually closed his eyes.

As Boo sat watching Carl, trance begot trance. Eventually Boo began to cast his eyes around aware that something was different. Something had changed. Something had come unmoored. Something had passed out of being and something had been made new.

Their trances were broken by the most awful cacophony of grinding metal and glass. When the sounds ceased, Carl smiled over at Boo. "That should be that." He rose from his chair and motioned Boo toward the door.

Opening the door, both men were hit by a blast of hot, humid air. The Etta Lee had come to rest a good two feet above the driveway, and she seemed to tip slightly as the two men stood at the open door. Carl jumped down. Boo hesitated momentarily gauging the rocking movement of the bob-house and then took a leap.

Almost as soon as snow boots hit pavement, voices call out, "Carl, who's your friend?"

"Ladies, this is, Boo!" Carl called out to the ladies who had gathered by the end of their driveway. "And he's unattached!"

Unzipping his snowsuit, Carl headed inside the house. As he passed through the front door, he turned sideways to allow two kids to rush out to see the cause of the clatter. Carl knew somehow they were Amy, a freshly graduated high-school senior, and Steve, a jaded college junior enrolled at Florida State. Inside, Etta was sitting at the breakfast table drinking a mug of iced tea, a deep scowl shrouding her face.

"What's wrong?"

"Amy convinced me to try this matcha tea. It's awful!"

"But you're ok? You're not sick?" Etta gave Carl a puzzled look.

"I think I'll be sick if I drink any more of this tea."

The kids stormed back into the kitchen each one shouting over the other. "Mom! Mom! Wait'll you see your car?!!"

Carl smiled.

All My Monsters

Some people believe in monsters; some people don't. But the funny thing is all monsters believe in people. You believe in what you need.

I didn't have my first monster until I was six. Up to that time we lived in Brooklyn and I had a Teutonic nanny named Lisel. Then Lisel left. Without explanation. We moved out to New London so my father could build submarines for the Navy. We bought a house previously owned by two creative sailors. And, of course, a vampire lived in the basement behind the heating oil tank. His name was Raul Chimichanga. I never saw him; I just sensed his brooding, malevolent presence. He never spoke to me but I knew the usual things about him. Like his name. It was just his name. And I knew it to be true the moment I sensed his foul corrosive soul. And his royal lineage. He was a Viscount and he owned a castle in Translavoburgh. And he had lightning speed and superhuman strength—as long as he was in shadow. In fact, he was physically constrained by the shadow border. He inhabited a prison with walls made of light instead of stone. If you turned the lights on he would disappear behind the oil tank faster than you could say "spawn of Satan."

Chimichanga was very suave and sophisticated—continental, in fact. I always suspected that he had something to do with Lisel's disappearance—the fact that she didn't come with us to Connecticut. Why else would she not have made the move with us?

Chimichanga had a special focus on me, precisely because I was not susceptible to his thrall. I was a challenge. His powers of seduction would surely work on the unsuspecting females in our household, but not on me. To maintain that immunity, I never referred to him by his first name—too familiar. I might drop my guard. Consequently, he would have to use his superhuman strength if he hoped to overpower me. And he could only do so under cover of darkness. As long as I had light, his powers were almost completely diminished and he was neutralized. That's how I kept him at bay behind the oil tank.

My father seemed to know all of this, though he never spoke of it. It was clear in the way he used the basement.

The previous owners had partially finished the basement. The finished part included the stairs along with a bar, a pool table, and a very adult seating area furnished with plush carpet and curvy throw pillows. The finished part also had several windows along two outer walls. They let in enough natural light that Viscount Chimichanga could never spend any meaningful time there except maybe for new moons.

If you came down the basement stairs and turned right, you went through a concealed door into the unfinished area. Immediately inside the door there were three concrete steps down and one small window, and in front of that window was my mother's sewing area. She had a new electric Singer sewing machine and one of those pin cushions that looked like a tomato with a picture of Lisel's face taped across it and a boatload of pins stuck in it. Two big hat pins pierced her eyes. It made me smile. In the middle of the room stood the fixture that gave the room its name—the furnace room—or as I liked to call it, Casa de Chimichanga. Storage shelves stood along one side wall. Past the furnace stood a four-by-eight-foot table with a plywood top on which I built and ran my train sets—the Glacier Express and the Orient Express. On the far wall, farthest from the door and the window, stood my father's workbench and Chimichanga's oil tank. Three bare light bulbs with pull strings lit the room—one above my mother's sewing table, one above my train table, and one above my father's workbench. The furnace room was Chimichanga's dark realm. Only the most diligent and masterful maneuvering on my part would allow me safe entry and egress. The slightest lapse of judgment or momentary distraction would mean the end of me.

It should be understood that my father never worked at his workbench. As Lisel had taught me to sing, "Ist das nicht ein Schnitzelbank? Ja, das ist ein Schnitzelbank." As far as I was aware, he never schnitzeled at that bank. (Nor did he ever ask me to have a catch or go fishing, now that I think about it.) His workbench was simply a place to display his tools—the tools that I was supposed to not touch. It was an altar to temptation—an opportunity for me to incur wrath. I was sure that on many occasions Chimichanga in fact *blatantly* touched my father's workbench in the dark of night and *intentionally* left tools conspicuously out of place. I swear he framed me on more than one occasion. It should also be noted that the placement of my train table and the installation of my train set on said table were almost certainly intended to lure me into the farthest, darkest recesses of the basement from which, possibly—just possibly—I might never return.

Constraining Viscount Chimichanga with light was very taxing, especially at the age of six. Upon entering Casa de Chimichanga from the door at the bottom of the stairs, I stood in a triangle of light that cut from the bottom of the door and across my mother's sewing table and chair. It cut through the darkness like a knife blade separating pure light from deepest darkness. I would have to scramble up on the chair in order to reach the light string. Reaching for the string, I could never tell what might be immediately to my right. Chimichanga? One of his minions? As soon as I pulled that chain, I reflexively turned to my right in case I might need to fend off some attack from the depths of hell. Some danger might be lurking ready to pounce upon me. By pulling that string, I gained an additional arc of light, a small addition to my operating arena. I could then safely venture beyond the furnace to the illuminated edge of my train table —but no further. As I pushed bravely to the edge of the light, I could make out shapes in the deep greys beyond. I always expected to catch a glimmer of Chimichanga's burning red eyes, but he never tripped up.

In order to operate safely around the entirety of my train table, I needed to turn on that light above it. That required jumping up and leaning forward over the table and swiping at the string like a little Nureyev. This often required multiple attempts. If I failed to complete this maneuver the first time, I would retreat huffing and puffing to the safety of my mother's sewing table before trying again. I would catch my breath as I waited for the string to stop swinging. Eventually, I became quite adept at this leap-and-lunge maneuver, and as time passed, gaining a few inches in height helped considerably. Having turned on the light above the table, I could safely navigate most of the basement. For added peace of mind, I would then turn on the light above my father's Schnitzelbank. With that light, the remaining shadows were greatly reduced, leaving Chimichanga well confined. Still, that did not prevent me from feeling I had the crosshairs of his incendiary rage on my chest or my back.

Exiting the room was an even greater hazard. Leaving a light on was a grave sin, so I would have no option but to face it. Often, after losing track of time, I would look up and realize that all was now dark outside that lone window. And if anyone else had come in or out of any part of the basement, they had probably turned off the light in the stairway on their way back up. So it was always a trial by darkness: first turning off the light over my father's workbench, knowing that in so doing I was giving Chimichanga more leash; then performing my grand jete to turn off the light over my trains, which if successful left me landing in encroaching shadows; and then sprinting past the sewing table and attempting to reach the string with a quick jump, landing on my feet in what might be total darkness. Then there were two options to make my exit. I could back out the whole way, which was slow and left me susceptible to sneak attack from some overlooked network of shadow. Or I could make a mad dash, counting on my speed to stay ahead of the dying of the light. Either way, I had to deal with the possibility that upon turning to exit the room and head up the stairs, I might have to face a dark stairway completely unlit at the top. I could well be heading directly into the clutches of Chimichanga or one of his drudges of darkness.

This was what I faced until about the age of ten, when the fascination of trains gradually faded. My sense of Chimichanga's constant presence also began to fade, and yet there were days when, entering the furnace room, I knew I was facing pure evil and I would once again have to rely on all my well-drilled leaps and shakes to get in and out safely.

Chimichanga virtually disappeared in my eleventh year when a new force exerted its influence on me. I had suddenly acquired superpowers. Hairs had sprouted—at first individual hairs, and eventually bolder collections of hairs. But not on my head. And my body gained the ability to change dimensions. Muscles appeared where there had been none. Sensations began to pulse from body parts that had never before communicated directly with my brain. I grew four inches one summer and Chimichanga packed up his bags and left town, perhaps in search of Lisel.

But another monster moved in. Unlike Chimichanga, the new occupant had free range of movement. His only limitations, such as they were, were certain transformations triggered by moonlight. His appearances were strategic. His name was Cinzano. He had been an Italian professional cyclist who had several first-place finishes in the Tour de France, the Giro d'Italia, and the Svenska Mästerskapen i Cykling to his credit. He was wealthy beyond belief from his Tour winnings. And he was a werewolf.

Stop asking me how I knew his name and his curriculum vitae. I just did. When first I became aware of his presence, he was ranging throughout the entire basement. I would see his footprints, fingerprints, and pawprints far beyond the limits of our basement. Though I'd never spoken with him, I knew the sound of his voice—both in human form and lupine. I knew his laugh—his raucous, confident but suave laugh. I knew his mannerisms with a cocktail glass, his way of cowing others in conversational banter, and his way with the ladies. He was everything I had to become at this stage of my life.

From him I learned the desirable sports to play at prep school (whatever prep school was)—crew and football, but more importantly individual sports like skiing, squash, and golf. If my prep school didn't field teams in any of those sports, I could take them up when I got to my elite eastern university. It's also good to be a Rhodes Scholar or at least go to Oxford or Cambridge for a term. And if I didn't get into an elite eastern university or win a Rhodes Scholarship, then it would be worthwhile to spend as much time as possible in those places in order to throw names around and make people think I did. And if you happen to come across a sweatshirt or blazer from one of those institutions, grab it. It would be bad manners for the owner of it to fuss over clothes, so finders keepers. It didn't matter that I knew nothing about prep schools or elite eastern universities or Oxford or Cambridge or Rhodes. I only knew they were things you threw around to suitably impress. And God forbid that you should ever correct anyone who mistakenly assumes you attended schools with names that ring out loudly like Eton, Exeter, Andover, or any other old English town. The ultimate in bad taste.

From him I learned the proper attire for every occasion. From him I learned the proper glassware and bar stock required for a stylish party. From him I learned the best way to treat people by beginning every conversation with the assumption that everyone you talk to is beneath you but may have something you want—especially women. Well, obviously women. Also, the best way to deal with people is to take what you want. Again, obviously women.

But Cinzano's core was alcohol, which burned brightly as his idol of idols. Everything began and ended with alcohol. It was the key to his confidence, his attitude, his disdain for others, and his dismissive boldness with women. I learned this lesson at an early age. I snuck into the basement bar at an early age. It didn't hurt that my father's familiarity had nurtured neglect for the finished basement with its bar, its pool table, and it's adult-themed conversation pit. My father never seemed to spend spare time at home anymore. Despite the décor being of the wrong decade, it was otherwise perfectly accommodating, and the whimsical decorations began to take on more and more meaning. I began by tasting each of the liquors and liqueurs individually when the parents were not at home. Then I went through the mixology manual my father had supplied the bar with, trying each concoction—again when the parents were not at home. I began increasingly calling them *the* parents instead of *my* parents, and they were increasingly not at home. This gave me a slight headstart when my classmates began attending house parties. In a matter of five years, I was one of the leading house party attendees, coordinators, facilitators, and raconteurs. I could boast being a functioning alcoholic at fourteen, thanks to Cinzano's tutelage.

Cinzano worked hard and played hard. His laugh could always be heard above the crowd and his behavior was over-the-top as well. He was the wild man, the master of excess, the priest of the bacchanalia. But his "hospitality" quickly lost its charm. His sexual charisma, real or imagined, soon proved to be void of the intended worldly allure. All of his antics eventually played out in missed appointments, sullied events, and alienated potential partners. But this transpired over the course of a decade or so—too slowly for me to notice until it was too late.

Another side of him was playing out behind the scenes. The spirit of the wolf would come over me—at first, when I was alone. And in the strangest places. In the shower. In my bed. In any place I was unobserved. Things would catch my eye. Lotions. Bath oils. Moistened wipes. And did I wipe! At first this pursuit was fed by the shear fascination of what my body was revealing to me. But it was soon prompted by the Intimates section of the JC Penney Big Book or the Virginia Slims ad in someone's Red Book magazine. The TV Guide sometimes served as trigger with Suzanne Somers or Jacqueline Smith on the cover; it ended up disappearing prematurely. Attesting to the fact that Chimichanga had been ousted, my train table was now collecting dust, but behind the papier mache mountain I kept a stash of prompts. Listening closely for any opening doors or approaching footsteps, I would go right up to the edge of Chimichanga's realm between the train table and the oil tank and perform my offering to the gods of fleshly delights. I was dead set on being fluent and adept with the equipment when I was called upon to use it. But alas, despite my constant practice and enthusiastic trials of novel applications, no call was forthcoming. I eventually realized that my longstanding relationship with Cinzano was actually falling short of my objectives. And gradually another voice began to woo me away from my cycling superstar's intoxicated three-ring circus.

In a rare season of clarity, I realized that I was lucky to have a job and I was lucky enough to be good at that job. And just at that moment, a new boss drifted into my cubicle and introduced himself. My new boss was the world's best boss. His name was Stillwagon, Charles Stillwagon. He was a self-made man—the kind no one can stand unless they're on their team. He would stick his head into my cube and say, "Attaboy!" Or passing me on the way to the men's room, he'd give me a "Go get 'em, tiger!" He gave me an exorbitant raise from next-to-nothing to next-to-nothing-plus-ten-percent. People began to notice me. I was going places—with velocity! The fat old ladies in Accounting began to invite me to their casserole lunches. I never attended, but I noticed who did: the young women who were destined to become fat old ladies. And I noticed the places where everyone else ate lunch when the ladies in Accounting brought in there casseroles. Men went to the company cafeteria. Anorexic women just went to the ladies room. And the rest took their brown bag lunches to the concrete benches encircling the CEO's Zen garden under the gaze of his corner-office windows. I was a company man, and I was going places. Stillwagon made sure of that.

Apparently, Stillwagon was a necromancer. He cast his deathly spells over everyone in the company. Those who displeased him faded away without anyone seeming to notice. But it became clear to everyone still working at the company whom he favored. I for one tried to be the first person in the office every morning. At first, I would see Stillwagon's car next to the car of the CEO, John Levolor, in the parking lot when I arrived. After a while, I would just see Stillwagon's car. Then without notice, Levolor disappeared and the next day Stillwagon was measuring the corner office for drapes. Within the week, Stillwagon became CEO—and he took me with him. By now I was making *four* times nothing with big percentage bonuses. I would hit the company gym and make a show of using the stair-climber. I had ambition and gumption and you could take it to the bank! It was no time before I had dated every coed on the company softball team, and everyone thought it natural when I asked the director of HR to marry me. What better place to propose than the Zen garden outside the CEO's office windows? What better place to formalize our nuptials than the CEO's horse ranch? And where better to take our honeymoon than an exotic resort where no one we know had ever been before? So, we sailed to Tierra del Fuego and camped out in the exclusive luxury of a three-room yurt equipped with sauna, jacuzzi, and his-and-hers bidets. When we returned from our paradise (where no one had been before and no one would ever go again) Stillwagon's sorcery went into over-drive—full-on FOLO—Fear Of Losing Out. We became wraiths running after anything anyone around us was doing or talking about or raving about. Following his example, we bought a house that we could afford to buy but could not afford to furnish; we bought matching blue and pink Lamborghini Diablo's and then tried to learn how to a drive manual transmission; and not too quickly we had two kids that we couldn't take care of. Then lightning struck. One morning as I sat at the light in front of the office, smiling to myself because I saw only Stillwagon's car parked in front of the building, the light turned green. As I shifted gears and stalled out, seven black SUVs swarmed around me with lights and sirens. Stillwagon was perp-walked out of the building. He'd been arrested for insider trading. For the next six weeks, agents from the FBI and the IRS roamed the halls like the Empire's Storm Troopers. We tip-toed through the office like mice skirting the walls, like Jedi knights under the shadow of the Death Star. And then axes rained from the skies. Jobs flew out the windows with a great sucking sound. When the terminations reached us, we began the day driving our two cars to work and ended the day driving our two cars back home. I pulled into the driveway. My wife had been fired before me. Her car was sitting in the middle of the driveway with the driver's door open and the key-in-ignition alarm ding-ding-dinging. I found her in the kitchen annex.

"I fired Sigrid," she said. She looked shell-shocked.

"You fired Sigrid?" I shot back. "Why? Who'll take care of the kids?"

"We'll figure something out," she said, "I guess." She looked lost. "But first we have to figure out what we're going to eat."

"You fired Brigitte, too?"

"Don't worry. We'll figure out how to get our dry cleaning."

I found her hope unconvincing.

The wife and I tumbled quickly down the ladder that we had so diligently climbed. It seemed our fate followed Stillwagon's headlines. *Stillwagon Indicted.* The general manager at Office Barn gave me the boot. *Stillwagon Arraigned.* The manager of the County State Credit Union rescinded the wife's job offer. *Stillwagon Trial Begins.* My manager at the Stop-n-Start announced that effective immediately all employees would have their positions demoted to assistant of whatever their position was with a twenty-percent cut in pay. *Stillwagon Convicted*. The wife was given a bad performance review for the drive-thru window. *Stillwagon Denied Parole.* I didn't even bother going in to work, afraid that I might owe them. The wife and I roamed the world like zombies, slowly shedding club memberships and timeshares, retirement accounts and tax shelters, until we were bare bones, down to one used smart car and one checking account. We enrolled our children in the Jehovah's Witness school which cost nothing but qualified for a tax deduction. We had reached rock-bottom.

Slowly we regained our bearings. I got a job with the State of Connecticut where I could draw on my depth of experience being fired and apply it to firing others. The wife found an opening with a non-profit—doing . . . something. Then before we knew it, our youngest reached eighteen. We put him and his sister in a rowboat and tried to launch them into the rip tide, hoping that they would mercifully meet their ultimate fate in Long Island Sound. They rowed back to shore and locked us out of our house.

That was the last straw for the wife. She passed shortly thereafter, succumbing to beaurocratoma or some other cancer of the cavity that's supposed to contain your heart.

That's when the last of my monsters came into my life. While enchanted, you don't notice the world around you except what satisfies whatever spell your under. You don't notice the world looking at you, watching you, casing you, examining you and your every move. Once my wife passed, I suddenly felt intensely naked in front of the world. That's when I noticed Skrindel.

Skrindel means "sneak" or "cheater" in the Old Norse language. And, no, I do not speak the Old Norse language, but you always know your monsters, including the meanings and origins of their names. Of course you do. You just do. Why wouldn't you? Come on, man!

Skrindel's single most distinctive trait was that he was always looking at me. But, as trolls often do, he had the ability to appear taller and wider at a distance, and shorter and thinner up close—like an afternoon shadow. At noon he could disappear under your shoe. He always appeared to be wearing two or three winter coats, even in summer. I would see him on park benches, staring at me. I would see him in shopping centers, staring at me. I would see him under parked cars, staring at me. As best as I could determine, he lived under a bridge with six other trolls. He had a trick of being able to fit himself into a shopping cart along with things he would collect in the course of his daily labors. He would con people out of their valuables, sneaking things away under their noses, sleight of hand with people's possessions, inveigling their rightful assets by luck, by hook, and by crook. I lived in constant fear of coming home one day and finding that Skrindel had taken possession of my apartment and its contents and changed the locks. Or receiving a letter in the mail notifying me that Skrindel had drained and closed my bank account.

I received a letter stating that the State of Connecticut had allowed a low-level bookkeeper to embezzle the entirety of my union's retirement fund. I could have been that low-level embezzler, but no such luck. My pension and those of every other employee of the State of Connecticut had been Skrindeled. The stockbroker with whom I had invested my small inheritance from my uncle had not served me well: Skrindeled. A disarmingly cute mutt got ahold of my wallet and proved to be much faster than I had expected: Skrindeled. When there is no longer anyone in this world who knows me or cares about me and I'm forced to sign over the last of my earthly possessions to some travesty of a nursing home: Skrindeled.

All our monsters, like all of our children, are created from the same stuff we're made from, spawned by us, and fed by us. They're what we want to be when we don't know any better or what we don't want to be when we still don't know any better. They're who we try to live vicariously through when we lack the gumption to give it a go. They're embodiments, projections, of what we lack or possess in excess. They resonate in the frequencies of our fears and fade in the presence of our best selves. Perhaps they're what others see in us or what we manage to hide. They are the earthly ties that we struggle to create at birth and so easily surrender at death. Where would I be without Chimichanga, Cizano, Stillwagon, or Skrindel? I wouldn't be the man I am today. Would I be better off—if I had the strength and courage to be who I was always meant to be. Or is that just for suckers? What could I expect, given that I never had what I needed growing up? Or did I just have the wrong response to needing?

Who took my shopping cart?

Siobhan's Gathering

The front door burst open. Conrad Doherty struggled to restrain the chocolate lab long enough to unclip his leash from his collar. Conrad turned to hang up the leash and grab a dog treat according to their routine, only to find himself waving a biscuit in thin air. The dog, once free, had trotted off purposefully toward the back of the house, his nails click-clacking as he progressed over the tile of the entryway and then along the hardwood of the center hall. Shrugging, Conrad put the unwanted biscuit down on the table by the door and sifted through the pile of mail. Finding nothing of interest, he turned to the right where his wife, Meg, was setting up the living room for company.

"Book club night already?"

"Yup."

He nodded with raised eyebrows. "What's up with Ziggy? He headed off like he had somewhere to be?"

"Your mother's room probably." She stood up, appraising the seating, the availability of coasters, the supply of napkins, dessert plates and forks around the boxed cheesecake, and a hard-cover copy of *East of Eden* on a plate stand with paperback copies directly under the table. She seemed satisfied with the preparations. "You know, it's the strangest thing. First thing this morning, I brought him in from his morning walk. He headed off to your mother's room and just stood at the door for a minute and then he pushed it open with his nose. He went in, sat down next to her bed, and put his head in her lap. Right in her lap." She cocked her head as if for punctuation, or perhaps demonstrating Ziggy's motions. "And he just stayed like that. For. Hours." She raised an eyebrow and paused, waiting for reaction.

"So?"

"I thought he must have smelled food in her room. I peeked in to check. No food. Your mother just sitting up in bed, stroking Ziggy with one hand. With her other hand, she was, like, waving it over the bed, like she was casting a spell or something. Very strange. Very. Strange."

"Why d'you say strange?"

"It was your mother," she said, pronouncing each word. "Your very . . . opinionated . . . mother."

"So?"

"I stuck my head in politely and asked if she needed anything. No, dear." Meg shook her head emphatically as she stepped closer to Conrad. "Then she said the strangest thing. She says, 'Look. Charlie came! And his leg is all healed! Like new.' "

"So?"

"Connie, there was no one there. And she said it like I could plainly see Charlie and his miraculously healed leg."

Conrad turned, looking off at the fireplace. "I think she was referring to Charlie, a spaniel she had as a child." Turning back to face Meg, Conrad continued, "My mother and my aunts used to tell this story about Charlie, this little dog that my mother loved. One day he got loose, ran off, they couldn't find him. He ends up getting hit by a car—or a wagon or trampled by a cow, depending who's telling the story—shatters his hip or his pelvis, and he makes it home dragging his hind legs. He goes to the front door yelping, and by the time someone came to the door he'd lost so much blood he that he died there on their front step."

The doorbell rang. Meg moved to answer it, saying as she walked toward the door, "Now you're the one not making any sense." She opened the door and ushered in the evening's first guest.

Conrad ducked out and headed to the first-floor bedroom that Siobhan occupied. There he found Ziggy just as Meg had described.

"Is Ziggy begging food from you, again?" he said as he gripped the door jamb, leaning his upper body into the room.

"Oh, Connie!" Siobhan looked up and smiled. "No, Zigs is just sitting with me. He's been sitting with me all day!"

It struck Connie that he hadn't seen his mother smile so brightly in quite a while—perhaps since his father passed five years earlier. "So, you're having a good day? Need anything?"

"A lovely day. No, nothing. Thanks, Connie, dear."

Conrad looked down at his mother's smiling face and thought to himself, "This is not my mother. No complaints. Not one pointed observation about someone else." Since coming to live with them, Siobhan had been a prickly tenant, a chore, a trial. He felt as if he were looking at the mother of his youth, of fond childhood memories, not the mother of his adulthood, not his widowed arthritic emphysemic complaint-ridden mother of recent years. As he was about to leave, he noticed Siobhan's left hand, twisted with arthritis, prone to shaking—now floating just as Meg had described, held out to her side, over the bed, moving steadily, steadily, as if resting on something, hovering over a small swirl in the bedspread.

The next morning, Meg entered Siobhan's room to find Ziggy once again at his station. Meg's attention to order was drawn to an open bedroom window. "Siobhan, did you open this window?"

"No. To be honest," her thin voice rose and then dropped weakly, "I don't really have the energy to be opening windows. I guess they wanted it opened. Maybe it makes it easier for them to come and go."

"They? Who they?"

"Meg, dear," Siobhan said, nodding her head as if choosing not to answer, as if sensing who was open to what realities. She then looked Meg square in the face. "I want you to know that you're going to wake up one morning with a sharp pain in your abdomen. Don't worry. It'll just be a kidney stone." She smiled gently. "Nothing to worry about."

"Siobhan?"

"Yes, dear?"

"What's our address?"

"Thirteen-oh-two Shrewsbury Boulevard."

"What's Conrad's middle name?"

"James."

"What month is it?"

"January, dear."

Meg looked at Siobhan without speaking for a moment and then left the room.

Standing looking through the dining room window out over the frost-trimmed front yard, Meg called Conrad's office. "Connie!"

"*What's wrong!*" came the thin voice in the earpiece.

"Something's going on with your mother. It's freaking me out! Did you leave one of her bedroom windows open?"

Hearing something in the house, she held the phone away from her ear. The tinny voice buzzed intermittently. She tried to isolate sounds coming from the front door. She thought she'd heard the latch. Continuing to listen in the quiet house, she could hear Siobhan exclaim, "Mandy!"

Putting the phone back up to her ear, she whispered loudly, "Connie, who's Mandy?"

Next morning, Meg was seated at the breakfast table. "Once again, after his walk, Ziggy came in, went straight to your mother's side." Meg watched Conrad's back as he poured coffee into his travel mug. She watched as he reached into the refrigerator and pulled out two slices of deli ham and a leaf of lettuce and threw them between two pieces of rye bread that he had placed on the cutting board. He slipped the sandwich into a used sandwich bag that he retrieved from his briefcase. "Conrad . . . why don't you—oh, never mind." He closed the bag, tossed it into his open briefcase, and slammed the case shut, clicking the latches. He sucked on the fingers of the hand that had retrieved the ham and lettuce, and then wiped the hand on a dishtowel. Meg raised her eyes to the ceiling. "As I was saying, apparently Charlie the invisible dog has made himself at home. And Mandy—who the hell is Mandy?—is coming and going at all hours."

"Well, don't worry about it. If she's not starting fires or joining a cult, what harm could she do? And if it puts her in a good mood . . ." Conrad picked up his briefcase, which as usual, contained little more than his lunch and random fast-food condiment packets. He leaned down to kiss Meg on the cheek and headed out the side door into the garage.

Meg heard the slam of the car door, the hum of the garage door opener, and watched as Conrad's tired SUV backed out of the driveway. A school bus applied its brakes loudly to avoid hitting him. He methodically stopped and then transitioned to forward motion. The bus lethargically resumed its route. Just as Meg was rising to clear the table, a blue minivan with faded roof paint and New York plates pulled into the driveway and stopped with a loud squeak, a knock, and a rattle. From where she stood, Meg could see two occupants—recognizable as Norene and Lyle—through the glint and mixed reflections on the windshield. "What now?" she said under her breath. Meg walked to the window, folding her arms over her chest, to watch with interest as the two got out of their minivan. They had no luggage, no gifts, nothing in hand. Had they been evicted? Running from the law? There's no telling with these two.

As they walked up the flagstone path to the front door, Meg moved to meet them at the door. Glancing toward the back of the house, Meg noticed—no Ziggy—despite the sounds of the minivan and car doors in the driveway. "Norene, Lyle! So nice to see you!" She hugged Norene.

"Unexpectedly." And in turn, Lyle. "Without calling first." They moved on through the entryway.

"Since when do I have to call first to see my own mother?" Norene asked rhetorically, shedding her coat like a molting crab. Norene worked as a "holistic teacher" at a private elementary school whose motto seemed to be "Learning Happens." Norene insisted it was officially "Where Real Learning Happens—Ubi Doctrina Vera Fit." But Meg had never seen any "Ubi" or any "Vera" on any school kit as much as she kept her eagle eye out for them. Lots of things happen, Meg thought to herself.

Already two steps down the center hall, Norene, walking backward, explained, "I just had to see Mom." She turned and proceeded to Siobhan's room. Lyle and Meg stood staring blankly at each other.

"Coffee?" Lyle half asked, half begged.

Meg nodded in resignation and gestured toward the kitchen. Meg deftly laid out two cups of coffee, bagels, cream cheese, a piece of cheesecake left over from her last book club meeting, and, as an afterthought, a two-day-old jelly donut.

"Megrit, you are the soul of hospitality." Lyle slid into one of the chairs at the table.

Meg smiled at his endearing, if presumptive, familiarity. At least he tried.

Once seated at the table with hot coffee mug in hand, Lyle reached for the jelly donut and began, "I got home from my shift at the hospital at 4:00 this morning. Norene meets me at the door, fully dressed, and says, 'I have to go see my mother. You can come or you can stay. But I've got to go see her.' I said to her, 'I've got another shift at 4:00 this afternoon.' She says, 'You'll be back in time.'" Lyle sipped the hot coffee, closed his eyes, and tilted his head back in deep, almost embarrassing, abandonment. "So, three hours later, here we are."

As the caffeine hit his blood stream, Meg saw light returning to his tired eyes. Lyle was a big man, not a fit man. A teddy bear. Well able to hoist a patient from a bathroom floor and into a hospital bed. "Lyle," Meg began, "What the hell is going on?"

"What the hell what? What d'ya mean?" He tilted his head questioningly, showing more animation.

"Two days ago, Ziggy went to Siobhan's room and basically hasn't left her side. Then *Charlie* showed up. And then Mandy, whoever she is. . ."

"Mandy's here?"

"Alright, who's Mandy?"

Lyle settled back into his chair. "Three-four years ago, Siobhan came to visit us the week of Norene's birthday. Remember that? You guys dropped her off and then the next week we brought her back?"

"Like a bad penny—sorry I shouldn't say those things." She slapped her hand in mock punishment. "Yeah, I remember."

"One night—it was after Norene's birthday dinner—I cooked and made a mess of it, but there was wine." Lyle nodded slowly. "We all got pretty loose. Siobhan starts talking about growing up on the farm and her mother and her sisters—Norene and Conrad's grandmother Tatya. And the two younger sisters, whatever their names were."

"Genevieve Adele and Sarah Lynn."

"Yuh. Genevvv and Sarrrr. And then she comes out with a bit Norene didn't know about: after Siobhan's birth, her mother had one more child—Amanda."

"And how did she hide this all these years?"

"Well, it was a home birth and the child only lived something like two weeks. And in those days, the state of Vermont didn't care if a child died in the first thirty days. So, Amanda was lost to history. But with Siobhan's mother bedridden for several weeks, little five-year-old Siobhan played nursemaid. Apparently, in that short time they developed a deep, deep," Lyle paused, stifling a burp, "deep bond. But she was so young she remembered very little of it. But with a little talk of the old days and a lot of wine—eh, you know."

Meg sat silent for a moment before speaking. "Siobhan's having a ghost party, is that what you're telling me?"

"Well, . . . they're coming for a reason." Lyle, leaning back in his chair, looked at Meg and then down at his coffee. "For the past two years, I've been on the pediatric floor, pediatric oncology in particular." Looking down at his coffee mug, he ran his finger around the lip of the mug. "Doctors rush in and out, but we orderlies, we sometimes hang around and get to see what really goes on with patients. On our floor, we have a therapy dog, Rosco, a beautiful golden." He slid the last piece of jelly donut into his efficient eating machine. "Rosco knows."

"Rosco knows what?"

"His handler says the dogs always know. They'll go right to a child that . . .that's about to die." Lyle took a deep breath. "He says their God's scouts, God's front line." Lyle looked significantly into his coffee and then deeply into Meg's eyes. "Before working pediatrics, I was on geriatrics for many years. It's a tough assignment. Well, one time we had a patient who had his rabbi visiting him frequently. I had a chance to talk with him a little. Rabbi Schmuli. Good ol' Rabbi Schmuli. At one point we got to talking about sitting shiva. He said that the Talmud tells us that the soul of a person mourns over its own body for seven days as well. The soul mourns because the body learned Torah and did mitzvahs in partnership with it, and yet the body's fate is to be buried in the earth while the soul soars to the heavens. And then he quoted I think it was Isaiah who says, 'He will swallow up death forever, and the Lord God will wipe away tears from all faces.'" Lyle paused. "'May it be speedily in our days,' he would say, 'May it be speedily in our days.'"

"What's that got to do with . . ." Conrad's SUV pulled into the driveway. Leaving his car in the driveway, he came to the front door, and entered. "Oh, hi, Lyle!" Without stopping, he proceeded toward the back of the house.

Meg looked at Lyle, mouthing an unspoken question.

Lyle looked off into the corner of the room, craning his neck. "Yeah, I've seen and heard some strange things." He turned to look at Meg. "Often an alert patient within a few days of death will start to look around, turning their head as if receiving guests or recognizing faces in a crowd, turning their head from place to place, nodding, smiling. In one case, a man—congestive heart failure—was approaching his time. He started staring into a mirror on the opposite wall and smiling. His daughter who was sitting by his side noticed it and looked into the mirror. I saw her just freeze. I asked her later what she saw. She said she saw her grandmother clear as day in that mirror under the fluorescents of a hospital room. Sure, a lot of patients, especially heavily medicated ones, drift off in their sleep. But even they often see people in the days before. I saw one gentleman, comatose for ten days after an auto accident, sit bolt upright out of the blue and shout, 'Mom!' and then pass away."

"Yeah, but isn't that mostly a neurological thing?" Meg asked meekly. "Isn't it just the brain firing off a lot of neurons, the electrical charge draining once the supply of oxygen is stopped? Like flipping a deck of flashcards before the lights go out?"

"Yeah, that happens." Lyle again focused on something beyond the window. "But that's really a matter of no more than three minutes. I'm talking about things that happen over several days. Something changes in their mindset, their physical being, their pheromones change." Looking back at Meg, Lyle shook his head. "No, that's definitely different altogether."

Lyle reached out and put his hand on Meg's. "In this life, we have the chance to pour our souls into the souls of others. When that happens, those souls become bonded. When it's time for someone to go, the soul starts to separate from the body, like a butterfly emerging from its chrysalis. When that starts to happen, those bonds, especially those to the other side, pull in souls who then come to watch over the passing. They will watch until the light comes. It's a deep bond, Conrad probably isn't even conscious of it. Norene is."

"What do you mean, 'until the light comes?'"

"Patients who have not moved in days will sit up and stretch out their arms. They will say, 'They're coming, angels of light,' or whatever their belief, whatever language they have for it. And then they see Jesus coming to pick them up. Maybe Jews are taken by Abraham, I don't know. But from what I've seen, if the light doesn't come for them." He looked off, unfocused again, out the window. He lowered his voice. "The darkness will."

Lyle put his mug down and looked at Meg. "I think it's about time." He rose from the table and nodded toward the back of the house. Looking down at Meg, "Come on. I've seen enough of these. It's almost time. We should go." Together they walked to the back of the house. Standing outside of Siobhan's room, they peered in. Siobhan had just leaned forward, looking upward out the window. In a frail, soft, peaceful voice, she said, "I see them. They're be-yoo-tiful. And He's come for me!" Ziggy beat his heavy tail against the carpeted floor, slowly. Siobhan's body fell back like a husk, audibly exhaling. Ziggy stood and sniffed her still gnarled hand once more and turned to look up at Conrad and then Meg. He walked out of the room and a minute later, Meg could hear him lapping from his water dish.

Liner Notes

When word leaked that **Doug Brown's second short story collection** had landed on the publisher's desk, the **excitement was palpable in the halls of Serif Press**. Knowing well the stories that had been already published elsewhere, speculation was rampant as to **which memorable character might grace the cover**: The fierce **Willum Strange**, the disruptive **Claudzilla**, or **Giacco** who disappeared people with a look. But how do you choose among monsters, ghouls, and mobsters to represent the lot of them? And now we know—**Gladfind**, a monster in form but not character, the one who rises from the laundry hamper to stand in the breach.

The other topic fueling the whisper chain was **which telltale tidbits**—which weirdness, bizarritie, and grotesquery in Doug Brown's story world—**were autobiographical**. The fanbase demands to know! Here's a run-down of what's been **fact-checked by the Doug Brown fanaticos**:

The Ghost of Grandma Herbert—The old girl with tits did in fact live downstairs. Doug Brown would watch her walk from the house to her car every chance he got.

On Toppa The Heap—The felonious events were largely autobiographical. Doug Brown moved from Paramus, New Jersey, not Providence, Rhode Island.

Spitfire—The events of summer were almost word for word, but Doug Brown did not get the girl. The setting for those events was moved twenty-five miles closer to Woostuh.

Pawns—Doug Brown watched the moon landing sitting very close to the TV. His vision never suffered.

Sailing the Etta Lee—Doug Brown has been accused of many things but has admitted to none.

All My Monsters—The portion involving Viscount Raul Chimichanga was 100% factual except that the vampire had no name and the Austrian nanny was not named Lisel but Anna Marie. And she married a dentist from Greenwich, Connecticut who divorced his wife rather than discharge the nanny.

Siobhan's Gathering—This story has no autobiographical content. It was drawn entirely from deathbed anecdotes, especially those common to multiple sources.

The **rumor mill** is already **whirring**—which characters are rife for sequel or serialization? Los fanaticos, please don't bicker! There'll be time to follow all storylines!

www.ingramcontent.com/pod-product-compliance
Lightning Source LLC
LaVergne TN
LVHW090603110826
845146LV00001B/249